# HOLD ME NOW

*Light My Fire Series*

## J.H. CROIX

This is a work of fiction. Names, characters, businesses, places, events and incidents are either the products of the author's imagination or used in a fictitious manner. Any resemblance to actual persons, living or dead, or actual events is purely coincidental.

Copyright © 2021 J.H. Croix

All rights reserved.

Cover design by Najla Qamber Designs

No part of this book may be reproduced in any form or by any electronic or mechanical means, including information storage and retrieval systems, without written permission from the author, except for the use of brief quotations in a book review.

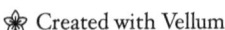 Created with Vellum

*To everyone who remembers we are all in this together.*

**Sign up for my newsletter for information on new releases & get a FREE copy of one of my books!**

http://jhcroixauthor.com/subscribe/

**Follow me!**
jhcroix@jhcroix.com
https://amazon.com/author/jhcroix
https://www.bookbub.com/authors/j-h-croix
https://www.facebook.com/jhcroix
https://www.instagram.com/jhcroix/

# HOLD ME NOW

*A brand new firefighter series from USA Today Bestselling Author J.H. Croix!*

**He's my new roommate.**
**I can't stand him, *and* he can't stand me.**

Russell Dane thinks he's *all* that. Maybe's he's so hot he should come with a too-hot-to-handle sign, but he drives me crazy. Not the good kind of crazy either.

He thinks women shouldn't be firefighters, he's obnoxiously overprotective, and I can't stand him. Unfortunately, my body is not getting the memo, but I'm stronger than a few confused hormones. Right?

It wouldn't be so bad if we didn't have to work together, and if he wasn't my boss. It definitely wouldn't be so bad if he hadn't gone and kissed me.

Russel & Paisley's story is perfect for readers who love small town romance, hotshot firefighters, sassy tomboy heroines, roommate romance, frenemies to lovers, hate to love, slow burn, emotional romance with a dash of angst, plenty of steam and swoon, and a broody, protective hero.

## Chapter One
# PAISLEY

My foot slipped on the edge of a rock, and I stumbled. Before I could take another step, I felt a hand on my elbow, steadying me.

Glancing back, I saw Russell Dane. I beat back the urge to shake his hand off and managed to say, "Thanks." I might've been gritting my teeth, but at least I was polite.

Even though my skin prickled from his nearness and I could hear every one of his footsteps, I tightened the strap on my backpack and kept walking. It irked me just to know Russell was behind me. I walked pretty quickly, but I barely cleared five feet, and he had to be at least six feet tall. By my guess, a slow pace for him meant a hustle for me.

I picked up my speed, only to come to a skidding stop when he said, "You don't need to rush on my account."

At my abrupt halt, his elbow bumped into my backpack. I spun around, narrowing my eyes. "Why don't you walk in front of me?"

His tongue pressed the inside of his cheek when he cocked his head to the side. I diligently ignored the inconvenient flare of heat between us. "No need," he said lightly.

Leaning my head back, I stared at the sky for a moment. I took a deep breath and let it out before I looked at him again. It was beyond annoying that I had to look up to meet his gaze.

His blue eyes stared back at me. "How many times do we have to go over this?" I pressed.

"Go over what?" he returned.

"Just treat me like one of the guys."

Russell narrowed his eyes at me. "I *am* treating you like one of the guys."

I shook my head. "No, you're not. You're obviously in a hurry, so just walk around me. That's what you'd do with anybody else on our crew."

Russell was another firefighter on my hotshot crew based in Alaska. We were headed back to the rendezvous point, where a helicopter would be picking us up. We'd been dealing with a wildfire in the backcountry. The fire was controlled, so our crew would be on our way home soon. Somehow, Russell ended up near me on our trek back. The rest of our crew was scattered along this trail as well, but most of them were behind us.

"Why does it annoy you to have me walking near you?" he asked.

I couldn't exactly answer truthfully. The honest answer was he drove me crazy, and I was so inconveniently attracted to him. He'd also been an asshole to me when I first got hired for this crew. He'd been all overprotective and shit. I did *not* need that. I'd been a hotshot firefighter for a few years before I moved here, so I had plenty of experience.

When I didn't answer, he rolled his eyes and quickly stepped around me. We began walking again. This time, I knew he was walking more slowly on purpose. Another minute later, I caught up to him. He stepped to the side of the trail, and I brushed by without a word. I wanted to say something, but a month ago, Graham, our crew superintendent, had forced us to have a conversation in his office because we'd had an argument. I'd never had a problem getting along with anyone I worked with. I loved this job, and I was falling in love with Alaska. Graham was a great boss. Here comes the "but"—*but* Russell drove me insane for all the wrong reasons.

I kept walking and resisted the urge to call over my shoulder and tell him to stop adjusting his pace to meet mine. I refused to speed up now and simply tolerated his presence behind me. Fortunately, we didn't have much farther to go.

I'd promised myself I wouldn't let him get to me anymore. It didn't make a bit of difference, but it took more effort than I'd ever admit. We made it back, and I was blessedly distracted by the others on our crew.

Phoebe sat down beside me on a log while we waited for the helicopter to arrive. She and I were the only women on the crew. Men dominated the ranks of firefighters, in general, but even more so in the world of hotshots. I was accustomed to that, but it was good to have another woman around.

Her blond ponytail swung when she brushed her hair away from her face. "Ready to go home?" she asked.

"Definitely," I replied. We'd been out in the wilderness for a week, and I had a deep hankering for a long hot shower.

Phoebe nodded, glancing over toward where

Russell was chatting with Graham. I reached into my backpack to fish out a water bottle. After I took several swallows, she commented, "You know, Russell has the hots for you."

"What?!" I sputtered. Her eyes twinkled when I glanced sideways. "You're joking, right?"

"Absolutely not. He was just staring at your mouth while you drank that water," she said dryly.

I wasn't about to fess up that I totally had the hots for him. Working as a firefighter, I was accustomed to the raw masculinity of the guys who did this kind of work. Most of them were rock-solid men, and they weren't jerks. With the exception of how he treated me, Russell wasn't either.

"I disagree," I finally said rather firmly. "He gets annoyed with me all the time."

"Yeah, that kind of proves my point."

"Well, it's a moot point because he annoys the hell out of me," I added.

Phoebe chuckled. "To my point again. I don't know you that well because we've only worked together for a month, but, uh, maybe it's a two-way street," she said lightly.

I rolled my eyes. "It's not. I'm not interested in relationships, in general, and specifically, not in anything with Russell."

She held a hand up. "Whatever. He's not my type, but he sure is easy on the eyes."

I knew my cheeks were getting hot, and I hoped the bright sunshine masked it. "More than one guy on this crew is easy on the eyes, but I don't have the hots for any of them."

She laughed again, stretching her legs out and crossing them at the ankles. "This isn't your first rodeo with a hotshot crew, is it?"

I shook my head. "I was on a crew in Washington for a while."

"You like the work then?"

"Definitely. This is your first job as a hotshot firefighter, right?"

Phoebe nodded. "Yeah, I did city firefighter work for a year in Seattle, but that's different."

I nodded. "Lots of hotshots start as regular firefighters. I was a volunteer firefighter in high school."

"Where are you from?" she asked.

"A small town in Washington. Are you from Seattle?"

I preferred that deflection to discussing my past. I loved my family, but there were too many complications at the moment.

She rested her hands on the log as she leaned back slightly. "I'm actually from Willow Brook. I moved away for college and stayed for a while."

"What brought you back?"

Something flickered in her eyes, but it disappeared. "I missed Alaska," she said simply.

"Alaska is definitely a far cry from Seattle," I said with a laugh.

Phoebe nodded emphatically. "I love Alaska. Have you ever been here before?"

"Nope. But I wanted to see it, so when I was scouting around to find another hotshot firefighter job and saw the opening, I jumped at the chance. Alaska has the most wilderness."

"There's even good coffee," Phoebe chimed in. "Firehouse Café makes some kick-ass coffee."

She was referring to a local coffee shop, which did, in fact, have excellent coffee. "Completely agree on that."

"There are also some good restaurants, and

Anchorage isn't far away if you need a dose of the city," she added.

The two helicopters arrived then, cutting off our conversation. I was relieved when Russell got in the other helicopter. I really needed to figure out how to deal with him. Originally, I'd blamed the tension between us on him. But now, I knew I was part of the problem. It rankled me to know that Phoebe had noticed there might be something between us. I had a hard time believing Russell had the hots for me, but she was spot-on when it came to me.

Why did he have to be so freaking handsome? He had those gorgeous eyes paired with rumpled golden hair. I didn't like that I'd even seen him without a shirt. That had been inconvenient for my hormones. One afternoon, I'd gone for a dip in a nearby lake. I'd thought no one else was around, and then he showed up. I'd ended up hiding in the trees to avoid him but gotten a nice long look at his glorious chest. And oh my, it was glorious, complete with a dusting of hair and a happy trail. Just recalling the view sent a wash of heat rolling through me. I did *not* need to be lusting after this guy, or even thinking about him.

Once we were in the air and closer to civilization, I turned on my phone to see if I had any messages. I was supposed to be moving into a new place this afternoon. I'd been making do at a bed and breakfast run by the woman who actually owned Firehouse Café. She'd cut me a break on the price, but it wasn't available much longer, so I'd been scouting around. Small towns didn't have many rentals, and I wasn't in a place to buy something yet. Janet had sent me to a local woman who was renting out the upper floor of a duplex.

It was kind of a weird setup. I was sort of a roommate, but not really. I had the entire upper floor to myself but would be sharing the kitchen area with whoever lived downstairs. I could totally deal with that. I was relieved to find a message from the owner and quickly replied to her text. *We're coming back this afternoon. I should land in an hour. Do I need to meet with you?*

My phone vibrated seconds after I hit send on that text. *I left the upper floor unlocked. Go on in. Welcome home, and welcome to Willow Brook.*

I smiled to myself. After we landed, I headed to the B&B to pick up the bag that was already packed. Within a half an hour, I was looking around my small apartment. It was super cute. A major bonus was that it came furnished. My footsteps echoed as I walked around the spacious living room with windows facing the lake.

The landlady had even left a set of clean sheets folded on top of the quilt. I smiled as I pulled out my phone and tapped out another text. *Thank you for the bedding. I haven't had any time to get to the store, so that's a nice surprise.*

*There are towels too!* she replied.

I quickly took off my dirty clothes and smiled as I tossed them in the washer—my very own washer. Ah, this was heaven. A short while later, I was showered and changed into clean, dry clothes. The only thing I needed to do now was figure out the food situation. I settled on ordering a pizza. That was perfect for tonight. I would go grocery shopping tomorrow since I had three whole days off.

Roughly twenty minutes later, there was a knock on my door. I'd expected them to wait at the shared entryway, but whatever. I leaped up from the couch, reaching for the cash I'd set on the coffee table for the pizza delivery person. When I swung the door open, the cash fell from my fingers, fluttering to the floor. Russell stood there with a pizza box in hand. His eyes widened the moment they landed on me.

## Chapter Two
# RUSSELL

Paisley Banks stood in front of me. Her auburn hair was damp and drying in wisps around her freckled cheeks when her hazel eyes met mine. Her cheeks flushed pink as we stared at each other. I finally shifted my brain into gear.

"Is this yours?" I asked, lifting the pizza box resting on my palm.

She nodded. "You deliver pizza?" She turned to bend over and pick up the cash that had fallen to the floor.

Of course, that action gave me a way too up close and personal view of her. She was wearing these fitted sweatpants, and the cotton stretched over her heart-shaped bottom. I had to yank my eyes away. It was bad enough that I could hardly keep my shit together around her at work, and now, she apparently lived upstairs.

My mother had just told me last week that she'd found a tenant for this place. I should've thought to ask her who it was when she said Janet recommended the person. Fuck my life. This was not good.

Paisley straightened. "I don't deliver pizza," I finally answered. "I paid for it because I thought it was mine. I should've realized it got here sooner than expected."

"How do you know it's mine?" She lifted her hand, brushing one of those wispy curls away from her eyes.

"Because I definitely didn't order a half pepperoni, half Greek pizza."

She smiled a little at that. "Oh. Well, I'll pay you, and then you can pay for your pizza."

I shook my head. "Nope. It's on me."

She pressed her lips in a tight line. "Russell, you don't need to pay for my pizza. Do you live here?" she asked, looking a little flustered.

She was rarely shaken. That shouldn't have given me a jolt of satisfaction, but it did.

"Yeah." I thumbed over my shoulder toward the stairs. "I'm downstairs."

"Oh." I still had the pizza in my hand, and we were still staring at each other. "Wow. This oughta be fun. I'll talk to the owner. I'm sure I can find somewhere else to move," she said quickly.

Now, I felt like an ass. "No, the owner is my mother, by the way. She'll kill me if she thinks you're moving out because of me, so that's out of the question."

## Chapter Three
## PAISLEY

"Um, okay," I said slowly, mostly because I didn't know what else to say. "Your mom didn't mention who you were."

When the doorbell rang, Russell turned and jogged down the stairs. I followed, thinking it was his pizza, but it turned out to be a package delivery.

He left the box by the door and walked into the kitchen, setting my box of pizza on the counter. Turning back, he rested his hips against the counter and crossed his arms. Instantly, I felt the way I did back at my interview. He'd given off intense vibes of skepticism. I'd left that interview thinking he was a sexist asshole. He was still a sexist asshole to me. I was pretty sure it was just me. He wasn't that way with Phoebe or Susannah, another hotshot firefighter at the station.

"How did you find out about this place?" he asked.

"Janet gave me your mom's number. I was staying at her B&B, but she's got it rented out to somebody else for the winter."

Russell nodded slowly. "Well, you're upstairs, and

I'm downstairs. The only space we have to share is the kitchen. There's still a TV up there, right?"

I almost laughed aloud because he looked slightly panicked about that. I cleared my throat and nodded. "Yes, that's part of the reason I jumped on this when I heard about it. It's furnished, and there's a television. I didn't bring much with me when I moved here."

His eyes, piercing and dark, felt like a laser beam on me. "Why did you move to Alaska? If you don't mind me asking."

I did, in fact, mind him asking, but it wasn't because of him. That was all on me, but I wasn't about to get into that with him. "I wanted a change of pace, and I love the outdoors. Anyone who loves the outdoors knows that Alaska is the crown jewel of the wilderness. When I saw this open position, I applied. I know you didn't want them to hire me." As soon as that last part slipped out, I wanted to snatch the words back.

Russell was shaking his head. "Not true."

"Don't bullshit me, Russell," I countered. At that moment, my stomach growled, and his lips kicked up in a smile.

His smiles were dangerous, and thankfully, he rarely directed them at me personally. For the most part, he seemed like a friendly guy around the station and with the rest of our crew. Ever since Graham had forced us to chat, he'd been scrupulously polite with me.

"I suppose you'd like to eat," he commented.

"Well, yeah," I replied with a shrug.

"I'll give you the quick kitchen tour," he began, just as there was another knock on the door. "That must be my pizza." He smiled again.

This time, my belly executed a quick flip, all

atwitter with excitement at a smile from Russell. Not one, but two whole smiles. I seriously needed to figure out somewhere else to live. I didn't think I could keep my sanity if I tried to stay here with him. That elicited a sigh because it was a really nice place. It was perfect for me.

Another moment later, he was waving off the pizza delivery guy. "Thanks," he called as he closed the door. Turning back, I noticed he had two boxes of pizza in hand.

"Two pizzas?" I asked.

He gave me grin number three, looking a little sheepish. "I eat a lot, and it's great to have leftover pizza. Wouldn't you agree?" I nodded because, of course, leftover pizza was great. "Now, let me finish that kitchen tour."

He set his boxes of pizza on the counter beside mine. He began opening cabinets and drawers and pointing out what was where. I had silently decided I was going to take my pizza back upstairs, but before I could do that, he pulled out two plates and asked me if I wanted something to drink.

I didn't need to create more tension between us by refusing that. Surely, I could handle sitting down and eating pizza with him. A few minutes later, I found myself sitting across from him at the round table. It was situated in a bay window that offered a pretty view of the lake with moonlight glittering over the water in the darkness.

"What lake is that?" I asked as I took out a piece of pizza and reached for a napkin from the stack in the center of the table.

"Lupine Lake."

"It's beautiful."

He nodded while he chewed on a bite of pizza.

"Considering how hard it is to find a rental around here, your mom didn't ask many questions."

His lips kicked up in a half-smile, sending my belly into a shimmy. "That's my mom for you. She trusts everybody."

I felt myself bristling, and before I could hold it back, I said, "You think I'm not worth trusting?"

Russell had been in the middle of lifting a slice of his pepperoni pizza to his mouth, and he lowered it. His eyes narrowed as he looked at me across the table. My body felt as if sparks were bouncing around inside, colliding with each other and setting little bonfires everywhere. Trying to live with Russell was out of the question. I'd probably go crazy.

## Chapter Four
## RUSSELL

Paisley stared at me across the table, her eyes almost daring me. She lifted her chin a little, and I tried not to notice the pink tinge on her cheeks. I definitely tried not to notice her full lips and those freckles dusted across her nose.

Fuck me. How was I supposed to deal with Paisley living here?

Paisley cleared her throat, bringing my attention back to her question. I had to reach to remember what she'd asked. She was *that* distracting.

"That comment wasn't about you. It was about my mother. She's the kind of person who takes in strays—animal, human, or otherwise. I'm not implying you're a stray or that I don't trust you. But leave it to my mom to rent out this room without bothering to mention to you who I was."

"She didn't tell you she was renting it out?" Paisley squeaked.

I shook my head. "She's rented it out before, but she usually lets me know. This time, she told me after the fact. She's good friends with Janet, so I'm guessing

Janet let her know you were looking for a place. As I'm sure you've already figured out, rentals aren't easy to come by around here."

"Yeah, I figured that out," she replied dryly.

"We'll make it work. Have you had pizza from here before?" I asked.

Paisley lifted a slice of pizza, shaking her head before she took a bite.

"It's a newer restaurant in town, and they'd better not ever close," I said.

She took a bite, closing her eyes after she finished chewing. She opened them, offering, "It's delicious."

"Right?"

We ate in silence for a few minutes before she asked, "Do restaurants come and go around here often?"

I wiggled my free hand back and forth. "Sort of. Alaska's weird when it comes to the economy. Even in less populated areas like here, a lot of tourists visit from spring through fall. Sometimes, places open with a plan to cater to tourists. That works in some areas, mostly the busier towns where cruise ships dock. Willow Brook is sort of an in-between town. We're not too isolated, and we're close to Anchorage, but cruise ships can't get here. So, places need to plan to cater to locals. Pretty sure this place will stick around because locals are their main business. Speaking of staying, what's your plan? You just doing some firefighter-see-the-world kind of thing?"

She finished chewing and took a swallow of water. "Is that a thing?" A smile teased the corners of her mouth.

I shook my head. "Nah, I made it up. Hotshot firefighting isn't for everyone, though."

I was more curious than I should've been about

her answer. I was more curious about *everything* about Paisley than I should've been.

"I love the area so far. I don't have a firm plan, but it all depends on how things work out. I like our crew so far."

I figured I might as well be honest. "Now that I'm not being a cranky ass, you mean?"

Her cheeks went a little pink, sending a jolt of lust down my spine. "It's okay. I snapped at you too. We sorted it out, right?"

"After Graham made us talk," I reminded her with a wink.

She laughed a little before glancing down at her plate. I opened my mouth to explain further, but I snapped it shut. I was relieved she wasn't looking my way then. I couldn't exactly tell her I was seriously in lust with her, and she was distracting as all hell. Because that would be crazy. I was pretty sure she couldn't stand me. Her eyes lifted again, and she nodded. "I hope so. I really want this to work out."

I shifted gears in our conversation, figuring it was best not to dwell on the tension between us. "Alaska is full of transplants."

Her brows hitched up in question. "Transplants?"

"People who move here from out of state and make it their home. Some people are running from something and figure they'll get far enough away here. Others just love the wilderness."

"Oh."

That one word had an edge to it, and it piqued my curiosity. Paisley didn't seem like the kind of person with a problematic past. I knew she was as clean as a whistle as far as her background went. Before we even interviewed her, they ran a background check on her. She didn't even have a speeding ticket on her record.

Although, she was obviously daring. One had to be, as a hotshot firefighter. She was also thorough and careful when we were out in the field. As much as I didn't want to admit it, my mind kept cataloging details about her.

"I'm going to see how it goes. I'm used to the winter because the Cascades in Washington get plenty cold. If things work out, I might stay."

We got through dinner, and I actually relaxed a little, which was a miracle, considering Paisley left me tied up in knots physically. After we finished eating, she asked if there was an assigned section for her in the refrigerator.

All I said was, "Just take the bottom shelf," because I knew it was empty. With just me here lately, I didn't need all the space available, although I enjoyed cooking. Thanks to my mother's insistence, I was a pretty good cook. But life was busy, and I didn't have time to cook often. Cooking for myself also tends to make me feel lonely.

"Thanks for having dinner with me," Paisley said. "Oh, and I'll pay you back for that pizza."

I shook my head quickly. "No need." Paisley opened her mouth to protest. "Seriously. My mom would lecture me."

She blinked up at me. For just one second, I wanted to close that distance between us and kiss her lush mouth. But I had enough control to keep my feet where they were and didn't move, not an inch.

Paisley cocked her head to the side, a glint entering her eyes. "So if I want something, I just need to mention your mom. Is that how it works?"

"Well now, I think you're teasing me, Paisley. Don't go crazy."

She bit her lip, and her cheeks flushed again. "I

won't." She paused, glancing down where she traced her toes in a circle on the floor before looking back at me. "Honestly, if it's weird for me to be here, please just say so. I'll find a way to back out of it with your mom so she doesn't hold it against you." At that, she practically dashed out of the kitchen and up the stairs, calling, "Good night!"

I took a breath and rested my hips against the counter, running a hand through my hair. It would be fine for her to be here, but holy hell, I needed to quench this relentless desire for her. She'd been with the crew about a month, and I'd only become more attuned to her with each passing day.

Leaning my head back, I stared up at the ceiling, muttering, "Fuck."

The ceiling had no answer. In fact, it rather felt as if the ceiling were mocking me. My mother had been on my case about a relationship lately. I felt like I'd been thrown back into the era when mothers hounded their sons to find a good marriage and paired them off with whoever had the best dowry.

When I'd shared that with my mother, she'd glared at me. "No, it's just, you're a nice man, and I don't understand why you hardly date."

I hewed to uncomplicated, casual relationships. I'd let it slip, and things had gone a little further with one woman last summer. I should've known better. She'd graciously accepted my explanation that I wasn't looking for a relationship. Even though she'd insisted we could stick with our arrangement, I hadn't wanted to string her along. It was already getting awkward.

I snagged a beer out of the fridge and went downstairs. The house was built into a sloping hill with the main entrance to the home on the center floor. My parents used to rent this house out with the central floor offering a shared kitchen and half-bath, and the upper and lower floors set up as two private apartments, each with a living room, bedroom, and full bathroom.

I made sure to close the door to my apartment and kicked my feet up on the coffee table. Beer in hand, I flipped through the TV channels and tried to forget Paisley was in the same building. It was to no avail.

Later on, I found myself in bed thinking about her plump lips and the way her T-shirt stretched across her breasts. Before I knew it, my hand slid over the aching length of my arousal. I found my release swiftly with Paisley filling my thoughts.

## Chapter Five
# PAISLEY

The following morning, I tiptoed down the stairs, pausing at the bottom and holding my breath as I listened for any motion in the kitchen. There wasn't a peep, so I finally mustered up the courage to peek into the kitchen. Finding no sign of Russell, I hustled outside.

After I climbed into my car, I realized he must have arrived last night after I'd gotten here. I experienced a stab of disappointment that he didn't know what kind of vehicle I owned. Seeing as we worked together and parked in the same parking lot, I knew what he drove. But maybe there was more to it than that. I tried to think if I knew what any other people drove. I'd recognize Maisie's vehicle because I'd seen her arrive. Aside from that, I was only familiar with Russell's truck. What did that mean?

"Now, you're being ridiculous," I said to myself as I started my car.

Once I turned out of the driveway, I headed toward Firehouse Café because I needed coffee. I was trying to figure out a way to tell Janet I needed another option for a rental. I already knew there weren't any. If she hadn't already rented the B&B for the winter, I think she would've let me stay.

I jumped out of my car and walked quickly across the parking area, my breath misting in the cool morning air. The bell above the door gave its friendly jingle as I stepped inside, the low hum of voices reaching me instantly. Even though it was early, this place was already busy. I waited in line, and my stomach growled audibly. When I got to the counter a moment later, Janet grinned. "Shall we start with your food order?"

"Please. How about two bagels with smoked salmon cream cheese? I'll have one now and then one at lunch."

"You got it." She called my order over her shoulder and then looked back at me. "Coffee?"

I paused, contemplating what I wanted. "Can you do that mocha thing you made me the other day?"

"You got it. No sugar, though, right?"

"Definitely not. I don't like my coffee sweet, but your mocha with that touch of chocolate is perfect."

Janet smiled as she rang me up and began to prep my coffee. "So, are you all settled?"

"Yep. It's a nice place. I didn't know Russell lived there." I'd abandoned the idea of asking her about other options since I knew she'd offered me the only one she knew of.

When her eyes met mine, I could've sworn I saw a glint of calculation, but it disappeared as swiftly as I imagined it, and she didn't say another word. She simply shrugged. "He lives downstairs, and you've got the upstairs all to yourself. You work with him, so sharing the kitchen shouldn't be a problem. Russell's a nice guy."

Janet's tone was a little too innocent, but I didn't know her well enough to call her out on it yet. "His mom seems really nice."

Janet nodded. "She is, and she could use that rental money."

I decided to push it a little. "Are you sure? Because it doesn't seem like she was renting it out before, and rentals are pretty hard to come by around here."

Janet looked the slightest bit guilty. "You needed a place to stay, and his mother mentioned it."

As I nodded, I heard the bell over the door jingle again and reflexively looked over my shoulder to see Maisie Steele walking in with her husband, Beck. Maisie worked as the dispatcher at Willow Brook Fire & Rescue and was becoming a friend, or so I hoped. Their hands were linked, and I couldn't help but take in how cute they were as a couple—Maisie with her brown curls and freckled cheeks and Beck with his rumpled dark curls and flashing green eyes.

"Well, hey," Maisie said when she stopped beside me at the counter, releasing Beck's hand. "Are you all situated in your new spot?"

"How did you know I was moving last night?"

"Janet told me."

"Where are you staying?" Beck asked. "Not easy to find a rental around here this time of year."

"Is it ever easy?" I returned.

"Definitely not." He chuckled.

"I didn't know it when I rented it, but I'm staying in the upstairs apartment where Russell lives."

"Oh, that's a sweet spot." Beck nodded. "Their family used to rent that out every summer to tourists, but they don't do that anymore, not since his dad passed."

He went quiet for a moment, almost like a brief

gust of cold air passing through the conversation. There was a story there, but I sure as hell didn't know what it was. I simply nodded. "Well, it's a nice place."

Janet handed me my coffee. "Your bagels will be out in a minute."

I waited at the end of the counter, and Maisie came to stand with me while Beck ordered. "I'm so glad you found a place. I don't know what I would have done if I didn't have a place right off when I moved here."

"What do you mean?"

"I inherited my grandmother's old house and her job too. I was kind of a bitch when I first moved here. I think it's a good thing they felt bad for me and gave me the job anyway," she offered matter-of-factly.

I sputtered on a sip of coffee. "Seriously?"

She shrugged. "Oh, I can be moody." She paused, glancing at Beck when he stepped forward to wait with us. "Right?"

"What?" Beck prompted in return as he immediately reached for her hand.

"I was kind of a bitch when I first started working at the station," she explained.

Beck's eyes bounced from Maisie to me and back again. He appeared to be attempting to assess the situation. She smiled encouragingly when his eyes met hers again. "It's okay. You can be honest."

His lips kicked up into a grin, and he nodded. "I thought she hated me. Secretly, she wanted me bad."

Maisie rolled her eyes. "So cocky."

I laughed, thinking about how obvious their love for each other was. They had a warm, teasing relationship. "You can be a bitch if it helps to adjust to moving here," Beck commented. "Although that doesn't really seem like your speed." I opened my mouth to say something when he added, "Well, except when it comes to Russell. You're gonna have to figure that out now that you two are roommates."

"We've already figured it out," I ground out, trying not to grit my teeth.

He nodded. "Good then."

Maisie met my eyes, a knowing glint in hers, but I ignored it and was relieved to hear Janet call my name when she set a small paper bag on the counter. "I'm sure I'll see you two back at the station." With a wave, I snatched the bag and practically ran out of the café.

## Chapter Six
# RUSSELL

"Herman's in a tree. Again." Maisie's eyes twinkled as she looked at me from where she sat at the reception desk. She covered dispatch and functioned as the control center for both the police and fire crews.

"Of course he is. That happens on the regular," I replied. We were discussing Herman, the cat that belonged to Carrie Dodge, an elderly woman who called over for cat rescues whenever Herman and her younger cat got themselves into a fix. "Isn't he getting old?" I mused.

Maisie shrugged. "I'm sure he is, which means he's probably half-blind."

I dipped my chin in agreement. "True. Where's the town crew?"

"They're out dealing with a fire. That's why I'm asking you," Maisie explained.

Graham appeared in the front and heard the tail end of our conversation. "I asked her to ask you," he said.

I glanced over with a grin. "All right, all right. Anybody going with me?"

"Paisley," Graham replied, just as the woman in question came through the swinging door from the hallway into the front area behind him.

Her smile was careful, but then Paisley was always careful when it came to me. I felt a prickle of awareness chase up my spine, immediately followed by the inconvenient desire that sizzled through me whenever I saw her. Annoyance came on the heels of lust because that was apparently how I coped with this awkward and inconvenient attraction.

I hoped my smile was as bland as hers. "You might as well help me rescue Herman. It's a regular thing for the town crew, but they're dealing with a fire."

Paisley nodded. "That's why I asked her to go," Graham added—*unnecessarily*, I thought—when I met his eyes.

I could've sworn there was a knowing glint there, but I ignored it. There was no way he could have picked up on my raw lust for Paisley. He sure as hell didn't need to know about it because I was going to banish it firmly into nowhere land once and for all. We were practically living together now.

"Do we need our gear?" Paisley asked as I turned to leave through the front.

Maisie, Graham, and I replied in unison, "No."

Paisley looked amongst us, slightly puzzled. "Well, that was quick."

"We just need the cherry picker truck. Come on, we can ride together."

Maisie tossed me a set of keys from behind the desk. "All yours. Have fun." She immediately took a call, answering with, "Willow Brook Fire and Rescue, how can I help you?"

With a nod to Graham, I left with Paisley walking

beside me. As we approached the truck, she offered, "I can drive."

I should've thought about my answer before I said it. As was the case with Paisley almost all the time, I didn't. "No need. I got it."

She stopped walking, and I turned to glance back. "What?" she pressed. "Is this a guy thing where a woman can't drive the big boy truck?"

Annoyance pricked at me again. "It's not a big boy truck."

Paisley rested a hand on her hip, one brow arching up. "Really? They make trucks like this for kids to play with, but they're not just for boys."

I wanted to argue, but I refused to take the bait and simply handed the keys over. Her fingers brushed mine when she took them from me, and it felt like fire dancing over the surface of my skin.

A moment later, she had started the truck and pulled to the end of the parking area. "Where to?" she asked after a long moment.

"Oh, right. You haven't been to Carrie's place. Take a left and head toward Anchorage. She's just past the town proper on the main highway."

We drove in silence. My knees felt scrunched up because it was a bench seat, and Paisley was short. I wasn't about to say a word about it, though, because I knew if I did, she'd snap back at me. Hard.

"You can take the next left," I said a few minutes later, thinking this truck felt awfully small.

Not only were my knees crammed against the glove compartment, but the air felt loaded with a charge about to go off. I'd never even thought about the space inside this truck, and I'd ridden in it plenty of times with many people. But then, I was with Paisley. Basically, everything that made me uncomfortable was Paisley's fault, I decided.

The blinker sounded loud in the truck. She turned onto the road that would take us to Carrie's house. "So, who's Carrie?" she asked, her tone conversational and carefully polite.

"Carrie Dodge. Born and raised in Willow Brook. She has a nice spread out here. It's an old homestead." I paused before adding, "We've got about two miles to go. You'll see a mailbox. That's hers."

"When you say homestead, what do you mean?" Paisley interjected after she nodded in response to my comment.

"It's a carryover from the old legislation where people could stake a claim for a homestead as long as they cultivated some of the land. You can't do that anymore, but plenty of families ended up here that way before. Carrie has subdivided hers over the years, but she still has a lot of property. She and her husband have lived out here for as long as I can recall, and he passed away a while back. Her cat Herman has a penchant for climbing trees. We had to take her excavator away because one time, she tried to get him out herself in the excavator, and the excavator fell in a ditch. She didn't get hurt, but it was kind of a project to deal with."

Paisley glanced sideways, her eyes wide. "Are you serious?"

"Absolutely," I said, putting a hand over my heart and making the sign of the cross. "I'm not really sure how old she is, but she loves her cat, and he's adventurous. She doesn't even call the emergency line anymore. She just calls the main number and whoever's available goes out. Usually, it's the town crew, but we all help."

"I like that here," Paisley said after a moment.

"What do you mean?"

"In some areas, hotshot crews can be kind of snooty. It *is* a different kind of work than town firefighting, but I figure there's no need to be territorial, especially when you're based in a town."

"Completely agree. We all pitch in."

"Is that it?" she asked next, pointing at the lone mailbox up ahead.

"Yep."

A few minutes later, we were parked in front of Carrie's house. She was waiting for us on the porch and waved as we climbed out. "He's over there." She pointed at a tree. When she looked back toward us, her eyes narrowed when they landed on Paisley. "I've never seen you before," Carrie said as she stepped off her porch and gingerly walked toward us. She insisted on not using a cane or walker, although she could've used some help with her balance. Fortunately, the ground was level, and Paisley moved as fast as I did to meet her halfway.

"This is Paisley," I said when we stopped in front of Carrie.

Carrie eyed Paisley and even cocked her head to the side as if she was trying to assess her. "You're not from Willow Brook."

"No, ma'am," Paisley said with a small smile.

"And you're another one of those girls who wants to be a firefighter."

Paisley laughed softly. "I *am* a firefighter."

Carry lifted her chin slightly before nodding. "That you are. I'm sure the women are better at it than the men anyway." With this, she gave me a dismissive wave.

I knew enough to keep my mouth shut. Paisley's

eyes slid to mine, and I saw the mirth glinting there. "So, who's handling the truck?" Carrie asked next.

I literally had to grit my teeth to stay quiet. Paisley surprised me by gesturing to me. "Why don't we let Russell do that part?"

"Herman's friendly when you get to him. I think he's going blind," Carrie offered.

"He made it up that tree," Paisley said as she eyed the cat where he was perched high in the tree. He let out an audible meow as he looked down at us. Paisley tossed me the keys, and I walked back to the truck.

Moments later, I was parked as close as I could get to the tree, and Paisley climbed in the cherry picker. It only took a few minutes before she had Herman in her arms. After I lowered the basket, Paisley climbed out and handed Herman to Carrie.

She began fussing over him, rubbing under his chin and murmuring against his fur. She smiled over at us. "Thank you. Would you like some cookies?"

Paisley looked surprised at that, but I wasn't. "We'd love some," I replied. "Do you have enough for me to take back to the station?" She often made cookies for the crews.

"I sure do. I have a fresh batch of chocolate chip cookies. Let me get Herman settled, and I'll be right out."

Paisley and I waited outside while Carrie returned Herman to the house. As soon as the door closed behind her, Paisley looked over at me. "Cookies?"

I grinned. "She likes making them. We like eating them."

"How often do we rescue her cat?"

"Maybe a few times a year. He's an explorer, you could say. I heard she got a kitten too, but I haven't been called out to rescue the kitten yet."

Paisley snorted, stuffing her hands in her pockets and idly tracing a circle in the gravel with the toe of her boot. Carrie returned and handed the cookies to Paisley, who commented, "Oh, these are still warm!"

Carrie smiled. "Keep that man in line," she called as we walked away.

I was about to toss the keys back to Paisley, but she surprised me by saying, "Why don't you drive? You don't need to squish your knees up against the glove compartment. I wasn't thinking about that when I offered to drive on the way here."

"I'll take you up on that." I chuckled.

Only seconds after we were back in the truck, the space felt crowded again. We were quiet for most of the drive, and I found myself struggling to make casual conversation. I needed to figure this shit out because she was sort of my roommate now.

"Sleep okay?" I heard myself asking, kicking myself mentally as soon as I did.

The minute I thought about sleep, I recalled how I had only fallen asleep last night by taking care of myself as thoughts of her filled my mind. Fuck me.

## Chapter Seven
## PAISLEY

Russell wanted to know how I slept? Answering that question required lying. Not that it was a big deal, but lying was a sore spot for me lately. I wasn't about to tell him that I'd had a restless night of sleep because I could hardly stop thinking about him. He'd crowded my dreams, and I woke up aroused. *Soooo* freaking annoying.

"Fine," I sort of squeaked. "The bed's comfortable."

Oh, Jesus. I was commenting on the bed.

"I know it's not a great situation for me to be there. We work together, and maybe it's weird for us to be roommates or whatever. I'll talk to your mom and make sure she doesn't think it's your responsibility. If you could just give me a little time to find another place, I'm sure it won't take too long." Now, there was another lie. I'd been looking since I'd landed in Willow Brook. Arriving at the tail end of the tourist season meant most places were already booked. I'd also learned many of them closed once the tourists left.

The silence following that felt loaded. Although it was hard for it to feel more loaded than the space inside this truck. The air felt the way it did before a storm when it was heavy with electricity. Any second now, lightning would sizzle through the air with a loud crack of thunder to follow. Maybe that would relieve the tension, although I doubted it.

I felt Russell's eyes on me when he glanced sideways as he slowed to turn onto the highway. My head turned on its own. The moment I collided with his gaze, it felt like a flame running up a fuse. I looked away quickly.

"It's really not necessary," he said. "We have an entire floor between us. I'm sure we can find a way to get along. We did eat pizza together last night without arguing." His laugh was dry.

I stared out the window. It was funny but not really. "We did," I finally said. When I looked back in his direction, his eyes were trained on the road again, and I was relieved. Eye contact with Russell was dangerous for my hormones. "I'll keep an eye out to see if any rentals open. If something comes along, I'll take it. In the meantime, I'll stay put."

I crossed my fingers where they sat in my lap and took a deep breath.

"Are you crossing your fingers?" he asked with a teasing lilt.

I whipped my gaze sideways, colliding with his eyes. I felt the flare of heat in my cheeks and shrugged. "Maybe I was. You're obviously used to having your own space. It's just—" I paused abruptly, gathering my thoughts. "We've already had some issues at work. I don't want to make things worse."

I didn't know how to read into his gaze. The look there was inscrutable and dark. He simply nodded. A few minutes later, we were back at Willow Brook Fire & Rescue, and I practically ran into the station, relieved to have other people around.

After work that evening, I went to the grocery store and got a few things. I was a notoriously bad cook. My poor mother tried to teach me, but it didn't help much. I liked good food as much as anyone. I just didn't seem to have the instinct for how to make it. I could handle the basics, but prepared foods were a godsend for me.

I didn't realize how tightly I was gripping the steering wheel when I drove down the driveway to my shared house. I hit a little bump and had to slow down and force myself to loosen my grip. I was worried Russell was going to be home, and I was really hoping he wouldn't. I was so attuned to his presence that I knew, even with an entire floor between us, there would be that subtle vibration of awareness humming through me. I let out a sigh of relief when his truck was not in the gravel parking area.

I hustled inside and put away my groceries and started to make macaroni and cheese. I had just set a pot of water on the stove when I heard the sound of tires on the gravel. My pulse sped up in anticipation. I tried, oh how I tried, to stay calm and cool inside. A minute later, he walked into the kitchen.

His eyes landed on me. "Hey there, what are you making?"

"Macaroni and cheese." His gaze bounced from me to the pot on the stove and then to the box.

"Out of a box?" he prompted, bringing his eyes back to mine.

I felt my cheeks get hot because apparently, I just got hot whenever I was around him. I nodded. "Yeah.

Is there a problem with that?" My tone sounded snappy.

"There's not a problem, but homemade mac and cheese is definitely way better."

He set some grocery bags down on the counter, and I watched in silence as he unloaded actual food. Aside from a few boxes of pasta, everything else was fresh. "Do you like to cook?" he asked after he finished putting everything away.

I was still stuck in place. When I realized that, I quickly stirred the pot of water. I hadn't even added the macaroni yet. Dear God. This man had reduced me to stirring water.

"I'm not that good at it," I finally said. I didn't see any sense in lying.

Russell blinked at me like he wasn't sure what I had said. "What do you mean you're not good at it?"

"I'm not good at cooking," I ground out. "That's why I make things out of the box. I get what I expect, and I can't really screw it up."

His brows hitched up. He definitely looked doubtful. "I suppose so," he said slowly. "Well, if you don't mind, I'm gonna make an actual meal."

I reached for the box. "This is an actual meal."

His lips twitched. "Sure, but homemade is better," he offered with a wink.

"Like I said, I'm not so good at cooking." I felt sheepish and annoyed. But annoyed was an almost constant state of being around Russell. I didn't even like considering the fact my annoyance was tangled up in my arousal. Just now, my belly was tingling as the heat bloomed through my body, and my pulse was galloping along faster than an excited pony.

"If you're in the mood for mac and cheese, I can make a homemade batch right now," he offered. "I can whip it up in about twenty minutes, and then it'll need time to bake."

I wanted to say no, I really did, but that felt rude. The man just offered to make me homemade mac and cheese, and I had to work with him. This was an excellent example of why it was such a bad idea for us to share space. "I'm not asking you to make me dinner," I mumbled.

"I know you're not asking. I offered." When he turned to look at me, I saw that familiar annoyance flashing in his eyes.

Sometimes, it felt like we were cymbals clanging against each other—*clash, clash, clash*—and I just wanted to relieve all that tension. I knew one surefire away to do it, but that was insane.

I finally shrugged. "If you'd like."

Russell leaned his head back, staring up at the ceiling. He leveled his gaze with mine again, replying, "I offered, and I'm cooking anyway. I have all the stuff to make it, so why don't we just do that?"

"We?" I questioned, my tone too sharp.

"Yes, that would be you and me. That's we," he explained patiently.

"Okay. Can I help?" I was feeling like a curmudgeon at this point. I also worried I was walking into a conversational trap.

"Sure, why don't you grate the cheese and boil water?" He gestured to the pot of water I had already put on the stove.

I realized I hadn't even turned the burner on yet. "I can handle that." I returned the box of prepared mac and cheese to the cabinet and turned on the burner.

He pulled out a cheese grater, setting it on the counter beside a giant block of cheese. Another moment later, he handed me a bowl. "You can shred it in there." He started to turn away but stopped and looked back at me. "Were you going to put a lid on the water?"

"It boils without it," I said, thinking I was stating the obvious.

Russell rolled his eyes. "It boils a lot faster with a lid." He got a lid out and plunked it down on top of the pot.

I was feeling even more snappish now. Annoyance rose inside me like a tide. It seemed to come in waves with him. "You know, I didn't ask you to make this."

"I know, I know," he said.

I recalled my mother trying to get me up to speed in the kitchen and often reminding me that I didn't pay attention to things I didn't like to do. The truth was, I didn't like to cook, and I always felt out of place in the kitchen.

"How much cheese should I grate?" I asked after I had opened it and rolled down the wrapping.

"About half that block."

I eyed the giant block of sharp cheddar cheese. "Half?"

Russell's eyes slid to mine. When his lips curled into a slow grin, my belly executed a joyous flip. "Yes, half. When I make mac and cheese, it needs a lot of cheese. No sense in skimping on it. It's the main ingredient."

I got to work grating the cheese, watching curiously as he got out another pan and started melting butter in it. Then he added flour and whisked it. I'd never watched anyone make homemade cheese sauce. Within minutes, he had added cream and then the cheese. He even added some spices. By that point, I had lost track of what he was doing. I sat down on the stool at the kitchen counter and decided to wait. He didn't seem to need my help.

After Russell assembled the macaroni and cheese in a baking pan, he sprinkled more cheese on top along with some breadcrumbs. He had assigned me the task of turning on the oven to heat it. Looking at the pan as he slid it in, I asked, "You don't just eat it? Everything in the pan is cooked."

Russell closed the oven door and set the timer before turning to face me. When he hooked a hand in his pocket, that subtle motion elicited the equivalent of an engine revving in my body. My pulse, which ran fast no matter what when I was near him, kicked up its pace even more. Because he put his hand in his pocket, drawing my eyes to the subtle flex of his forearm. Good Lord. This was ridiculous.

"No, I don't just eat it," he said slowly. "You need to bake it. It makes everything blend better. Plus, then we get the crispy on top. I'll have to make my crispy mac and cheese for you."

"Crispy mac and cheese? What's the difference?"

"I don't put it in a baking dish like that. I spread it across a cookie sheet. Everything bakes thin and crispy. It's tasty, especially if you're a fan of slightly burnt cheese."

"Wow. I never thought of that."

He chuckled, slipping his hand out of his pocket. Turning, he crossed to the refrigerator and opened it. "Want anything to drink? I have beer."

"I don't love beer," I said when he glanced over his shoulder.

"Do you *like* beer?" he pressed.

"Actually, no. I don't even think I like it." My cheeks were getting hot, and I didn't even know why.

He pulled out a beer for himself. "You don't mind if I have one, do you?"

I shook my head. "Of course not."

"I saw that you got some wine. You could have that." He gestured to the bottle of wine on the counter.

I grabbed on to that suggestion like it was a lifeline and I was drowning. I *was* drowning—in heat and lust. "Good idea." I slipped off the stool and trotted across the kitchen, fetching the bottle of wine.

Before I could even ask, he pointed at a cabinet beside the refrigerator. "Glasses are in there."

I pulled out a glass and filled it with wine, thinking I needed to find a way to disappear from the kitchen. But that seemed rude. He had just made dinner for me. I had grated the cheese and preheated the oven, but my contribution felt small. That pan of mac and cheese looked delicious, and I was beyond hungry. I just didn't know how long I could handle spending time with him.

I took a big gulp of wine, hoping it would take the edge off my nerves, which felt stripped raw around him. I was hypersensitive to every tiny thing he did. I jumped when the phone rang. Russell glanced my way as he stood from where he'd taken a seat at the table and went to answer it.

"Hello?" He listened, nodding. "Yeah, she's right here." Turning, he held out the phone.

"For me?" I asked.

"Says he's your brother."

I took a breath and hoped the alarm ringing like a gong inside my body wasn't obvious on my face.

## Chapter Eight
# PAISLEY

I set my wine glass on the counter and reached for the phone. "Hello?"

"Hey, sis. How's it going?" my brother replied.

"Okay. How did you get this number?" I was more curious than I wanted to be about that. I didn't even know it myself. I'd blocked my brother's number from my cell after I moved here.

"Mom gave me this number."

Now, that was a big fat lie. I knew it, and he knew it. The unease I'd become accustomed to living with concerning my brother slithered through me. "How are you?" I knew my tone was stilted, and I wanted to walk out of the kitchen. This whole thing was weird, and Russell obviously had no idea that I was barely on speaking terms with my brother for reasons that were confusing to me. Blessedly, Russell walked out of the kitchen, and I heard his footsteps moving down the stairs.

I let out a sigh. "What is it, Ryder? Why are you calling me?"

"I actually want to know how you're doing," he insisted.

"No, you don't. Please don't track me down like this."

"I already did."

"I know, and why?"

"Because I care about you, even if you don't think so," my brother insisted.

I gritted my teeth, clenching my free hand into a fist before opening it and shaking it to release the tension in my body. "Ryder, what do you need?"

"Nothing. I just called to give you a heads-up. If you hear from a guy named Tom Smith, let me know."

"Are you serious? Now you're warning me about people?"

Ryder was silent for several beats before he said, "Yes, I am."

"Tom Smith is probably a common name."

"I know, but you don't know one, or at least not that I'm aware of. If you hear from one, let me know right away."

"Ryder, what the hell is going on?"

"Nothing you need to know about."

"Well then, why the hell are you calling me?"

"I just told you."

Fuck. "What the hell is going on?" I repeated.

"Paisley, I love you. Maybe you're not thrilled with my choices, but I'm trying to make sure you're okay."

"Well, I thought I *was* okay. I moved a few thousand miles away."

"You didn't have to move away," my brother pointed out.

"I know I didn't, but I'm tired of trying to keep your secrets from Mom and Dad. That's on you now."

For the first time, I heard a twinge of guilt in my

brother's reply. "I know. I'll figure it out. This isn't going to go on forever. I promise."

I heard Russell's footsteps coming back up the stairs. "I'm glad you're doing okay. Thanks for calling." This was not a conversation I wanted to have at all, and most definitely not in front of Russell.

"You take care. I love you."

"Love you too." I set the phone back in the cradle on the wall beside the kitchen counter.

Turning away, I crossed to the island where I'd left my wine and reached for the glass. I took another gulp just as Russell returned to the kitchen. He was looking at something on his phone and had his beer in his other hand. He glanced up. "You didn't have to end that call on my account. You could have gone upstairs if you needed some privacy."

"I know. It was just my brother saying hello." *And warning me about some random guy.*

Russell nodded. "I didn't know you had a brother."

I shrugged. "How would you have known? We haven't talked that much."

His eyes narrowed as he took a long drag from his beer. My eyes trailed down to his throat, lingering on the motion as he swallowed. A shaft of heat slid through me. I took another swallow of wine, hoping my nerves would settle. That was probably a long shot, but a girl could hope. Between my reaction to Russell and that call from my brother, I was wired tight.

Oblivious to my state, he lowered his beer. "No, I don't suppose we have talked much."

"Do you have any brothers or sisters?" I asked as I crossed over to sit at the table. I might as well make polite conversation.

"No, it's just me. I'm an only child."

"Are you spoiled rotten?" I teased.

He shrugged. "Don't think so."

"You're from Willow Brook, right?"

"Yep. Born and raised here."

"What do your parents do?"

A shadow crossed over his eyes. For a flash, I thought his gaze held intense sadness, but it disappeared quickly. "My dad was a firefighter, but he died a year ago. My mom's a teacher." His voice was flat as he recited those facts.

My palm flew to my chest. "I'm so sorry. I didn't know."

"It's okay. You might've heard about it around the station because he used to be a firefighter on the town crew there."

"I'm so sorry, Russell. I really am."

"Me too," he said in a gruff whisper. He took another drag from his beer. "What about your parents?" he asked as he lowered the bottle and walked over to sit down across from me.

"They live in Washington. My dad's a lawyer, the local district attorney. It's a small town, but he's a big fish in a small pond. My mom's a florist. She loves flowers and gardening, so it suits her."

Russell nodded politely. "That's nice. What does your brother do?"

Ah, now that was a loaded question. I couldn't tell him the truth, so I told him the lie my brother told everybody. It wasn't a complete lie, but it definitely wasn't how he supported himself. "He's an accountant."

"That sounds boring," Russell offered with a grin.

I shrugged. "I suppose so."

"How did you end up a firefighter?"

I was so relieved he didn't linger on my brother that I didn't even mind talking about myself. "I signed up for a volunteer crew in high school and loved it. I decided to do my training to be a hotshot firefighter after college."

"What did you do in college?"

"I majored in land management. I love the outdoors, and I figure I won't be able to be a firefighter forever because it's hard work. I'll be able to do some kind of wildlife management job after that. At least that's what I hope."

Russell nodded. "Smart move."

"Did you go to college?"

"Yup, in Washington. Did the whole city thing in Seattle."

"Did you like it? I almost can't imagine you being in a city."

He cracked a grin, and butterflies spun in my belly as tingles radiated through me. It constantly felt like sparks were bouncing around inside when I was near him. When he was actually being nice to me, I worried those sparks would combust into a bonfire.

I thought perhaps I should start an argument, but I was too unsettled between my brother's call and Russell telling me his father died.

"I liked Seattle, but I wanted to come home. Moving away shows you what you want sometimes."

"I suppose so. I spent some time in Seattle too." When he arched a brow, I added, "That's where I went to college. University of Washington."

"You're kidding. When did you graduate?"

"Six years ago."

"I'll be damned. I must have been a senior there when you were a freshman."

"It's a big school. Definitely not the place where you'd meet everybody."

The sound of his low chuckle sent those butterflies

into a spin. At that moment, the kitchen timer went off, and he stood to walk over and glance in the oven. "It looks ready. You hungry?"

"Sure." I stood from the table. "Can I do anything?"

"You can get two bowls out." I crossed over to the cabinets and got out the bowls.

He spooned in the mac and cheese, and my mouth watered. He even brought over a bottle of some kind of spice when he carried the bowls over to the table. "You might enjoy a dash of chipotle." He cast a quick grin. "It's tasty."

I sprinkled some on mine, realizing at the last minute that I'd forgotten to get spoons. I jumped up and grabbed them out of the drawer before returning to the table.

"You have to take the first bite," he said from where he sat across from me.

Staring into his eyes, I felt my chest tighten, and my breaths were short.

"Um, okay." I lifted a spoonful, watching the steam rise and giving it a second to cool. As soon as my mouth closed over it, I let out a moan. The subtle smoky flavor of the chipotle mingling with the rich cheese and the crunch from the breadcrumbs and browned cheese on top was, simply put, heavenly. I moaned shamelessly again after I finished chewing, then opened my eyes. "Oh, my God. *That* is amazing."

Russell waggled his eyebrows and then took his own bite. "I told you it was better than the kind from the box," he said a moment later.

I held a hand up. "You will get no argument from me on that. You can cook for me every night, in fact."

"Now, now. Don't be saying I'm good at things. That might mess up our record."

"What record?"

His brows hitched up as he gave me a long look. "Of you telling me I screw things up all the time at work."

"I don't do that," I snapped, irritation rising inside.

"Yeah, you do. The other day, you got after me about how I started the chainsaw. Then you didn't like the perimeter I set when we were out last week." He shrugged, seeming unbothered as he took another bite of his food. I started to feel a little sheepish. "You even thought I walked too close to you the other day."

I narrowed my eyes. "You were too close. I know you were doing that to annoy me."

"No, I wasn't. I was just walking. My legs are a little longer than yours, in case you didn't notice."

"Obvious much?"

Russell threw his head back with a laugh at that.

I decided to focus on my food. I had a sneaky feeling he was right about me being so picky around him at work. After a few more bites, I offered, "This is amazing. Thank you."

"Anytime. I might not cook dinner for you every night, but if we're around at the same time, I'm not gonna let you make something from a box."

"I won't argue."

We actually finished eating and managed to have a normal conversation. Afterward, I cleaned up. I couldn't seem to get my nerves to settle. I didn't know what to think about my brother tracking down this phone number and warning me about that guy. I kept trying to forget about it, but I couldn't. There was that, and the other track in my mind was busy with my body's traitorous response to Russell.

He was actually being nice, and I felt sad about his father passing away.

What the hell was I going to do about this roommate situation? It was not ideal.

After I closed the dishwasher, I turned and rested my hips against the counter. As soon as I did, I realized Russell was standing right there, drying his hands on a towel.

My eyes fell to his forearms, watching as they flexed with the motions. For God's sake, the man was drying his hands. It was not supposed to be sexy. The second my eyes whipped up, heat flashed to my cheeks, and our gazes locked.

Russell was quiet. His hands lowered, and he carefully hung the towel over the handle on the stove directly across from me. When he turned back, he seemed to be considering something.

Meanwhile, I'd gone freaking crazy. Because I wasn't even thinking, and I'd taken a step closer to him. There couldn't have been more than six inches between us now. I could hear the rush of blood in my ears with every beat of my heart. My entire body was tingling with electricity.

Russell's eyes searched mine, and I wanted to say something, but I didn't know what to say. "What are you doing, Paisley?" he asked.

"I don't know." My voice came out a little breathless.

"You know what I want?"

I felt the motion of my head as I shook it. "No," I rasped.

He took a step closer, and suddenly, the air around us felt electrified. He was *right* there. I could actually feel the heat radiating from his body. "I want to kiss you, and that's probably not a good idea."

My brain thought it was a bad idea, but my

hormones were making such a racket, I couldn't listen to anything else. "Why not?" I whispered.

"Because we kind of can't stand each other. Although, maybe we can."

My mind blanked, and my palm landed on his chest. I could feel the thump of his heart beating against my hand. His eyes darkened, and everything felt blurry as if time was slow and fast at once. His head lowered, his eyes on mine the entire time. His gaze felt like a dare, and I never could back down from a dare.

I was leaning up to meet his lips just when they landed on mine. The subtle brush of his mouth was electrifying. The touch of his lips was soft and warm, and he rasped, "All you have to do is tell me to stop."

Well, there was no chance in hell of that. Not if my hormones had any say. I arched against him, letting out something like a whimper. I was not that girl. Whimpering was not a thing I did. But maybe it was with him.

The next thing I knew, Russell's palm was sliding down my back, his touch confident and hot. Just when I felt the tease of his fingers on the upper curve of my bottom, his hand swept up again. His fingers laced in my hair as he cupped the back of my neck and angled my head to the side. His mouth fit over mine with a firm, commanding sweep of his tongue.

I moaned shamelessly into our kiss. My fist was curling into his T-shirt, and the kiss just went on and on and on—lazy sweeps of his tongue and nips on my bottom lip. He dropped a kiss at one corner of my lips and then the other before he dived back in. It felt as if he was learning my mouth.

All the while, my body had a mind of its own. As I flexed into him, my nipples were tight and achy, and I could feel my arousal slick at the apex of my thighs. By the time he broke free, we were both gasping for air. My brain felt filled with static, and electricity traveled in a fiery circuit through my system.

Oh. My. God. I wanted this man.

Russell looked as startled as I felt. We stared at each other, wide-eyed and silent, save for the sound of our ragged breathing. He gave his head a hard shake and stepped away. I had to forcibly uncurl my hand from his shirt, and it fell against my leg.

"Oh, my god," I whispered before turning and fleeing the room.

## Chapter Nine
# RUSSELL

I stood in the kitchen, listening as Paisley's feet thumped on the stairs and the door slammed shut a few seconds later. I took a step back, sagging against the counter as I curled my hands around the edge because I needed something to hold on to.

What the hell had I done?

My body was on fire, and my cock was as hard as a baseball bat. I blinked, giving my head another shake. After a moment, I gathered myself enough to straighten and glance around the kitchen. Everything had been put away except my empty bottle of beer and Paisley's wine glass. I fetched the glass from the table and put it in the dishwasher. After starting the dishwasher, I rinsed my beer bottle and tossed it in the recycling bin under the sink. Then I walked downstairs, plunked onto the couch, and turned on the television.

The television wasn't an effective distraction. My mind kept replaying that crazy kiss with Paisley while my body pumped with adrenaline and need in the aftermath, like an electrical explosion scattering sparks after the initial burst. I eventually resorted to a cold shower and took care of myself, which was completely unsatisfying. The knowledge of how delectably good Paisley felt pressed against me kept me restless for most of the night. I knew that kiss was stupid, absolutely stupid. Fuck me.

---

When I woke up the following morning, Paisley was gone. My guess was she beat feet before the sun cleared the horizon so she didn't have to face me this morning. I wasn't sure if that was good or bad. On the one hand, I wanted to see her, yet I knew that was dangerous. I did *not* need to be getting tangled up with someone I worked with. Not to mention, we were usually annoyed with each other. That was our baseline.

To think we could somehow get along? I snorted, even contemplating that. I wasn't looking for a relationship, and I doubted she was. We sure as hell shouldn't have a fling. Talk about complicated. Maybe my body wanted her, but that didn't mean it was smart. I decided to leave early and grab breakfast at Firehouse Café. At least, I'd have somebody to talk to there and wouldn't be trapped in this mental replay loop of Paisley's kiss.

After a quick shower to wake me up and a short drive, I parked in front of Firehouse Café. The parking lot was already crowded, which wasn't unusual. Barely a second had passed when I walked through the door, and I *knew* Paisley was here. I hadn't seen her car. Hell, I hadn't even seen her yet, but it was as if my body was a compass, and she was magnetic north. I sensed her presence, and my head instantly swiveled to where she was sitting at a table by the window.

Maisie was seated across from her. The early morning sunlight fell through the window at an angle, gilding Paisley's auburn hair with a shimmer of gold. Everything in me tightened, and electricity sizzled through my body. As if she somehow knew I was there, her head turned, and her eyes locked with mine. We stared at each other for a long moment, and the hairs on my body stood, attenuated to her. My heart kicked hard and fast against my ribs, and I tore my eyes away. I walked and stood in line, relieved only two people were in front of me. I stuffed my hands in my pockets and stared up at the chalkboard menu mindlessly. I didn't need to read it because I already knew what I wanted.

When I reached the front of the line, Janet smiled at me. "Morning, Russell."

"Morning, Janet."

"What can I get for you?"

"Coffee, extra strong, and your egg, bacon, and cream cheese bagel thing, whatever that is."

"My egg extravaganza bagel?" Janet arched her brows in question.

I grinned. "Yes, that." I fished my wallet out of the inside pocket of my jacket and slipped out a twenty-dollar bill, laying it on the counter while she prepared my coffee.

She called over her shoulder to the kitchen, "An egg extravaganza, extra bacon and extra cheese."

"Thanks for remembering the extra cheese."

"You always like it with extra cheese." She winked.

"That I do."

"So, how are things?" She slid my coffee over, taking the cash and ringing me up.

"They're good."

"Your mom told me Paisley's staying upstairs at the lake house," she said conversationally.

Of course, Janet knew that since she was the one who suggested it. I had enough sense not to comment on that.

I nodded, keeping my reply nonchalant. "Yup."

"She settling in okay?"

My mind conjured the feel of Paisley's tongue gliding against mine and her warm curves pressing against my chest. My thoughts came to a screech, the sound audible in my mind. "As far as I know." I shrugged, attempting to cement how much it didn't matter to me who stayed there. "I'm in the downstairs apartment."

"You share the kitchen, though, right?"

Jesus. Janet was not going to quit with her questions. I nodded. "We do."

"Your mom always said you were a good cook, so make sure Paisley doesn't starve."

I chuckled at that. "I made her macaroni and cheese last night. She was about to make it out of a box."

Janet widened her eyes comically. "Oh no, the horror," she teased. She handed me my change, and I stuffed it in the tip jar.

"Don't tell my mom. I don't want her to hold it against Paisley," I teased in return.

"Why? Does she have something against prepared foods?"

"She never let me make them," I said dryly. "That's why I can cook."

Janet chuckled. "Well, you be nice to Paisley. She's new around here."

"I'm always nice," I muttered, feeling a little defensive.

Janet couldn't know that Paisley and I had been dealing with some tension at work. Although Janet seemed to know everything, even things people didn't tell her. She studied me for a moment before nodding. "I'll holler when your bagel's ready."

Someone had walked in behind me, so I scooted over to stand at the end of the counter. I took a swallow of my coffee. With the knowledge that Paisley was just across the café, my back was prickling with awareness. Uncertainty slithered through me, an unfamiliar feeling. I should walk over and say hello because I worked with Paisley and Maisie. I was overthinking this, and it was ridiculous. Maisie's voice reached my ears, and it prompted me into action.

I turned and strode over, schooling my expression to be neutral. "Morning, Maisie. Morning, Paisley," I began with a nod before taking another sip of my coffee.

Maisie smiled at me brightly. "Hey, Russell. I'm glad Paisley's renting the upstairs at your lake house."

"Yep, it's a nice little apartment." I didn't know exactly why, but I felt the need to clarify that it was actually a separate space. We had separate bedrooms, living rooms, and bathrooms. I didn't even want to think about having a shared bathroom with her. It was bad enough to have to share the kitchen. It was torture on my sanity.

Maisie glanced between us. "Are you two getting along better at work?"

Paisley sounded like she was choking, and I glanced down.

"You okay?" Maisie asked.

Paisley nodded before grabbing her coffee to take a

sip. I almost laughed, but I managed to stay quiet. I hoped maybe she felt as uncomfortable as me. Maisie looked up at me, pursing her lips, and I realized I hadn't answered her question. "Yep. We are. Why are you asking?"

I was feeling surly about the whole thing, annoyed that anyone around the station knew we'd been tense with each other. Maisie shrugged. The innocent look in her eyes was bullshit. I knew it, and she knew it. "No reason. I didn't know you had a problem with women firefighters."

When I made a grumbling sound, Maisie blinked. "Just joking. I know you don't."

Paisley looked from me to Maisie and back down at her bagel, her cheeks going a little pink. Good. Maybe she hadn't slept well last night either.

"What do you think of Alaska so far?" Maisie asked Paisley, blessedly dropping the topic of me and Paisley and work.

Paisley finished chewing a bite of her bagel before replying, "I like it. It's just as beautiful as I heard."

Janet called my name, and I interjected, "Gotta run. I'm sure I'll see you both at the station."

Normally, I would hang out, but I needed to get the hell away from Paisley, so I grabbed my egg extravaganza and hightailed it out of there. As soon as I walked into the station, we had a call out to a lodge that had caught fire a few hours north of Willow Brook. Thank fuck. I needed to work.

We were on the move within minutes. Anybody who wasn't already at the station was filtering in, grabbing their gear, and we were all heading out to the landing pad out back and piling into the two waiting helicopters. The sound of the helicopter blades whirring through the air drowned out everything else, and I leaned my head back to watch.

Not much later, we were dropping from the air, our gear heavy on our backs. We rolled into action once we were on the ground. In this case, the lodge itself was a lost cause, so we moved quickly to contain the fire by establishing perimeters, working until darkness fell.

That night, we all camped out. It was part of the job. I hated that I was acutely aware of where Paisley was whenever I wasn't deep in the middle of working. We kept our distance from each other, and that was probably for the best. The crew was big enough that it was possible to do that without it being obvious. The following morning, I woke when the first slivers of sunlight were reaching into the sky. The mountains were dark silhouettes against the silvery gray of dawn. I rose, my breath misting in the air. My boots scuffed the ground as I walked along the path to a narrow creek we'd come across the day before.

When I heard footsteps coming toward me, I didn't even have to lift my head to know it was Paisley. My body knew. The simple knowledge of her presence was a jolt to my system. I was still half asleep and not in the greatest mood because of that stupid kiss. I wasn't sleeping well, all thanks to Paisley. My head lifted, and our eyes collided. I could see her breath clouding in puffs in the air. Her cheeks were pink.

I was instantly annoyed because now I *knew* what it felt like to kiss her. It wasn't just a passing attraction. Hell no. It was fiery hot.

"Morning," I said, my voice coming out gruff and stilted.

"Good morning," she replied, her voice raspy.

As I got closer, my eyes took her in—the freckles

on her cheeks and the way her green eyes were so bright in the silvery light. It felt as if coils were twisting tighter and tighter in my body. She blinked and then brushed by me in silence. Great. Now we were back to this.

## Chapter Ten
## PAISLEY

I could hear the rushing *whoosh* of my pulse racing through my body. My breath was short, and my lungs felt tight. Meanwhile, my entire body was tingling with awareness. I could feel Russell's retreating form as he moved farther away. It felt like we were two magnetized forms in space. Everything in me wanted to turn back, to follow him and demand an explanation for why he'd kissed me the other night.

I wasn't blaming him entirely for that kiss. It was a two-way street. His head dipped down, and I leaned toward it. I had been powerless to stop it from happening. And now I was mad at him all over again. Because it shouldn't have felt so good. I was confused and annoyed. I'd known I was attracted to him before, but then he had to go and be such a good kisser. Like ridiculously good.

Meanwhile, I felt foolish because I didn't want to be this attracted to him. I had to find somewhere else to stay. I'd even asked Maisie about it yesterday morning, but she had no suggestions, like none. Neither did Janet. Fuck, fuck, fuck my life.

I stomped my way back to the small tent I shared with Phoebe, relieved to be working today. We'd be flying out soon because we had the fire mostly under control. Once we finished clearing a perimeter around it, air support would fly over with flame retardant.

The lodge had been burned to a crisp. We were coming into the end of fire season. Come fall, when people were hunting or camping, inexperienced people made bad decisions. No one had set this lodge on fire, but someone had a campfire nearby. There were the usual reasons for accidental wildfires in the backcountry, and Alaska was no exception in that regard. Campers being careless where they shouldn't was more common than it should've been.

I shook my head, ate a breakfast bar, had some kick-ass coffee, and then settled in for a hard day of work. I was worried because tonight I would be returning to the place I shared with Russell. Even though we only shared the kitchen, it felt *way* too close for my comfort.

---

At least I had the excuse of being exhausted when I got home that night. When I walked in, Russell was making some food in the kitchen, so I waved on my way upstairs. After taking a long shower, I was annoyed with myself for feeling so aware of his presence. It was ridiculous. He wasn't even on the same floor, and I locked the door. I needed to just forget he was here.

I was freaking starving, so I ordered pizza and camped out by the windows to wait for the delivery. I hurried downstairs to meet the guy at the doorway. I thought I'd escaped dealing with Russell, except when

I walked back into the entryway, he called out, "Avoiding me?"

I peered into the kitchen, shaking my head. "No. I'm just tired. I'm gonna have pizza upstairs. Is that a problem?"

"Nope, not a problem," he said with a shrug.

I scurried upstairs. I could've sworn I felt his presence chasing me up there. He was in the building, he was big, and his presence was potent. I ate pizza by myself. But I didn't have anything to drink, so I had to go down to the kitchen. I tiptoed my way down, relieved when he wasn't there.

My luck evaporated. I was filling a glass of water when I heard his footsteps on the stairs. "Fuck," I whispered.

A second later, he entered the kitchen. He put a plate and a glass in the dishwasher. The room was silent, and the space felt loaded as if a charge was hovering in the air and about to go off. I turned, and my eyes locked with his gaze immediately.

"How's it going?" I asked.

"Fine. We're heading into the quieter time of year as far as work."

I nodded. "Yeah, we are." The winter season was much quieter for hotshot firefighters. "How does it work in the winter around here?"

He shrugged. "We help out with any town calls, do backup for nearby areas, that kind of thing."

I didn't realize I hadn't responded until he asked, "You forgot to get some water?" His lips kicked up at one corner with his question.

It felt as if a thread connected us—his half-grin spread into a full one, and I felt a tug low in my belly. I literally felt his grin in my cells. I was suddenly breathless and tingling all over, but I managed to nod, feeling a little sheepish and hoping it didn't show. "I'm just going to go finish my pizza now." I scooted past him and practically ran up the stairs, feeling ridiculous about the whole thing.

I doubted he was as affected as I was by our kiss. Later on, I fell asleep, once again restless.

The following morning when I saw Russell in the kitchen, I was feeling contrary.

"Good morning," he greeted me when I crossed over to get a yogurt out of the refrigerator.

I felt obliged to respond. "Morning," I replied curtly.

"Is this how it's going to be?" he asked as I started to walk out.

"What do you mean?" I snapped, turning back to face him.

"This, the silent treatment," he clarified.

I shook my head. "I'm not giving you the silent treatment."

Russell stared at me, and it felt as if his eyes were boring through me, reading into all of my uncomfortable feelings. He somehow knew how unsettled I was by that stupid kiss and how it left me in a perpetual state of arousal and frustration around him.

"Really?" he drawled.

I narrowed my eyes. "Really. Do you hear me talking right this second? That's not silent."

He leaned his head back, letting out a dry chuckle before he brought his gaze to mine again. "I do hear you, but I think you're full of shit."

I rested a hand on my hip. "I'm not full of shit." My common sense had apparently fled the room because I moved to stand in front of him and actually wagged my finger at him. "I am *not* giving you the silent treatment," I said, enunciating each word carefully.

"Was it that kiss?" he asked.

Just hearing the word "kiss" aloud set little bonfires alight in my body. I took a breath, letting it out in a huff and wishing I could be all cool and nonchalant like him. "No, it's not that kiss. Although, for what it's worth, that was a mistake. I'm sure you'll agree with me."

He stared at me, and I wished I could read his mind. Something flickered in his eyes, but I didn't know how to interpret it. I didn't really know Russell all that well. I'd only been in town a short while. What little I'd been able to gather about him was that he tended to keep things casual with women. I wouldn't even call him a flirt because he wasn't. He didn't even have to be. He was so good-looking, it didn't matter. He was like honey to bees, him being the honey and women being the bees. And me. Apparently, *I* was a bee. I let out another huff, annoyed at my train of thought.

"What?" he pressed.

"Nothing," I snapped.

"I don't think the kiss was a mistake."

His words startled me, and my eyes flew wide as my mouth dropped open. His lips kicked up into a grin, and those bonfires spun in pinwheels through me as my belly executed a flip. I swallowed. "What?" My question slipped out in a whisper. I wasn't even sure what I was asking.

"Just what I said. I don't think that kiss was a mistake. It was a great kiss."

I felt as if he were daring me to argue the point. And, God help me, I never could resist a dare. I grew up with an older brother and spent most of my childhood trying to outdo him at every little thing. Maybe my brother had completely fucked his life up right now, and I was mad at him, but when we were little, I'd wanted to beat him at everything. I looked up to him that much.

I narrowed my eyes. "What is your point?"

"If that kiss was such a mistake, I dare you to kiss me again."

Oh. My. God. "You're daring me?" I sputtered, shocked.

He said the word aloud. "Yeah. If it's no big deal, just kiss me and prove that that kiss was bad."

"I didn't say that kiss was bad," I retorted, my words getting ahead of my brain. His grin spread to the other corner of his mouth. "That wasn't my point," I muttered, flustered with my reaction to him. "I said it was a mistake. That's different."

"A good kiss is a good kiss," he pointed out.

See, he was all cool, talking about that kiss like it was nothing. It was far more than nothing to me. I was no innocent virgin, but I hadn't had a ton of experience with relationships. I'd had other priorities. And, frankly, as far as I could tell, most men were a letdown beyond the superficial sheen.

"Whether or not it was a good kiss isn't the point. It was still a mistake," I clarified again, which promptly annoyed me even further.

I didn't need to keep clarifying that I hadn't said the kiss was bad, but he was implying that I had. For crying out loud, this was the definition of a conundrum. Well, that and the fact that I wanted this man. And it was a very, *very* bad idea for me to want him. We worked together, and now we lived together. Until I found another place to stay, I was in a bind.

He moved a step closer, and I shook my head wildly. "I can't, Russell."

His gaze sobered immediately. "Can't what?"

"I know this is all fun and games to you, but we work together. I'm new here, and I'd like to keep my job."

Of course, it only made matters worse when he immediately respected me. "Say no more." He held a hand up. "I'm sorry. You get under my skin, that's all. Can we at least *try* to be nice at work? I thought we were getting better for a bit there."

"Maybe for like three days." I lifted one shoulder in a slight shrug. He chuckled, and my pulse kicked up its heels in response. "I could try again," I offered, feeling flustered as heat flashed in my cheeks.

"Sounds good."

I started to turn away again when he commented, "Don't forget a spoon."

I snagged one out of the drawer nearby before hurrying back upstairs without another word. I closed my door, leaned my back against it, and let my hips slide to the floor. I ate my yogurt right there. Russell left me in a tizzy.

---

Not much later, I went in to work, telling myself not to get snappy. Halfway through the day, I had a phone message from my brother, which sent my mood plummeting. "No need to heed my earlier warning. Take care. Love you." The line went dead after that vague and brief message. I'd been walking down the hallway and stopped to lean against the wall.

"But why don't I need to heed your warning?" I asked my phone, idly wondering why blocking my brother's number didn't block the messages. They just showed up on my blocked list, which I freaking checked because I worried about him.

Obviously, my phone couldn't answer my question, and I knew my brother wouldn't tell me even if I asked. My best guess was whoever he'd warned me about was now in jail. Of all the things I'd worried about when I was growing up, my brother becoming a designer drug dealer had *not* been on that list. Instead, I'd worried about learning to fly like a bird and if our house was brick. In the category of out-of-the-blue childhood fears, for a while, I was afraid of our house burning down, and I thought bricks couldn't burn.

I leaned my head back and let out a sigh before pushing away from the wall. When I heard footsteps and looked up reflexively, my belly did a little jump and my pulse skittered wildly when I saw Russell. He had a smudge of dirt on his cheek. My eyes soaked him in greedily—the way his muscled arms swung easily, the way his shoulders filled out his shirt, and the way his cargo pants hung low on his hips. Jesus. I was getting hot and bothered looking at my co-worker slash roommate.

"How ya doin'?" Russell said easily, hopefully oblivious to my ogling.

His tone annoyed me. It wasn't him. It was just that he really wasn't as affected by me as I was by him, and it was so obvious. Well, that, and I was already feeling edgy after my brother's call.

"Fine, you?" I returned, my tone sharp.

Russell's brows hitched up slightly, and his eyes searched my face. "Ah, so that's how it is. Catch you later." He tapped my shoulder as he walked past me, and I had to fight the urge to shrug his touch away.

## Chapter Eleven
## RUSSELL

When Chase asked if I wanted to go to Wildlands, I immediately agreed. I sure as hell didn't want to go back to my place tonight. I didn't know what was up with Paisley, but she kept running hot and cold. She had a point about that kiss, and it rankled me a little. Because, holy hell, that had been one smokin' hot kiss. I didn't mind admitting to myself I wanted more, but it wasn't sensible. I knew it wasn't.

Chase had suggested going out together because we had a couple of new firefighters who'd joined the crew recently. Rowan Cole was the last one hired. He came by way of North Carolina and knew Remy Martin, who worked on another crew here.

Wildlands was a favorite hangout in town. It was a sprawling lodge on the shores of the lake. What had started as a small place had grown over the years, and now they had a kick-ass bar and restaurant with good food and good people. A hodgepodge of firefighters from different crews was here tonight.

I leaned back in my chair and took a long drag

from my beer before glancing toward Rowan. "So, what do you think of Alaska so far?"

He dipped his head with a quick smile. "I like it."

"You ready for winter?" Beck asked as he leaned his elbows on the table and stole one of Levi's fries.

Levi slid him a look. "I ordered those, you know."

"I know," Beck returned easily. "I ordered a basket too. You can have some of mine."

Levi rolled his eyes and pushed his basket to the middle of the table. "Everybody, help yourselves."

"Let's just all share appetizers. It's easier that way," Beck commented.

"Works for me." I pushed my basket of fried halibut bites to the center of the table and snagged a few fries.

"What's winter like where you're from?" Chase asked Rowan.

"We definitely have winter. I don't think it gets as cold in the Blue Ridge Mountains as it does here. We might get more ice, though, because we get the freeze-thaw thing all winter long. It's damn annoying," Rowan replied.

"We definitely get ice, but once winter hits, it stays pretty cold here. We get what we call snow roads. It's usually too cold for the salt to melt the ice."

Rowan's brows hitched up. "Damn, that's cold."

Levi chuckled. "You get used to it. If you can deal with hotshot firefighting in the mountains, you can deal with winter here. Plus, it's not like the northern part of Alaska, where it's dark all winter long. The days get shorter, but we don't lose the sun completely."

Rowan flashed a rare grin and nodded. He'd been with us about a month now, and I'd come to learn he was the quiet sort with flashes of humor here and there. He noticed every detail too. He was good with strategy when we had to plan quickly out in the field. "How'd you end up here again? You know Remy, right?"

Rowan nodded. "Yep. I know Remy and also Delilah Taylor."

"She's with Alex Blake," Beck commented.

"Yep. They met through Remy," Rowan confirmed.

"If you haven't met Nate Fox yet, he's one of the guys who flies us out to the backcountry sometimes. His wife, Holly, is Alex's twin sister," I offered.

Rowan nodded. "I met Holly when she came out to visit in North Carolina."

At that moment, Remy came walking by, pausing at our table. "Hey, guys." He clapped Rowan on the shoulder. "You doin' all right?"

Rowan looked up. "Doing great. These guys are telling me I can handle winter. You've done a North Carolina winter and now several here. What do you think?"

Remy chuckled. "Cold is cold is cold. Once it gets to a certain temperature, it's all the same to me."

"You joining us?" I asked.

Remy shook his head. "Nah, I'm having dinner with Rachel over in the restaurant. Speaking of, I better get over there, or I might be late." He spun away, walking backward and looking at Rowan. "You know where to reach me if you need anything."

"Small world. Seems like Alaska is full of transplants," Rowan observed.

"On firefighter crews, plenty of people move," Ward commented. "Might as well while you're young enough to handle the job."

Rowan nodded. "True story."

At that second, I heard a voice and felt a prickle on the back of my neck. Without even looking, I knew

Paisley had just walked in. Beck put two fingers between his teeth and whistled.

"Maisie here?" I asked with a grin.

He nodded. "Of course. I told her to meet us here. She's got Paisley and Susannah with her."

At that, Ward spun in his chair, a slow smile stretching across his face.

"Wait a minute, shouldn't you guys all be home with your kids?" I asked.

"Our kids are in the same place. When you have a good babysitter, you all take the night off," Beck replied.

Levi interjected, "Lucy's home. She didn't want to come out. I told her I wouldn't be late, though."

"Are you ever late going home?" I teased.

"Hell no. I try to stay on Lucy's good side at all times."

"I don't think it's that much trouble for you," Ward said with a chuckle.

Maisie appeared at the table with Susannah and Paisley, and we shuffled our chairs around. I was debating whether it was worse for her to sit beside me or across from me when Ward scooted over and patted the chair beside him. "Here you go."

Then there she was, immediately beside me. I glanced over, cautiously bracing myself for the jolt sure to hit my system. All I had to do was look at her, and my body felt struck by a fiery bolt of lightning. It was always hot and quick.

"How's it going?" I asked, thinking I should've known it wasn't safe to come out and meet the guys. Too many of them were paired up with women who'd befriended Paisley.

"Good," Paisley said, her tone curt.

"Have you been here before?" Susannah asked as

she leaned around Ward. Her strawberry curls bounced on her shoulders.

Paisley shook her head. "I've seen it, just hadn't gotten around to stopping here. It's always busy."

Susannah said something in response to Paisley, but I didn't even register it. Paisley's scent drifted up to me. I didn't know what the hell she washed her hair with. I'd never noticed the scent of a woman's hair before, but hers had this subtle berry smell. It was at odds with her tomboy look. And, somehow, that made it all the more appealing.

"Russell?" Ward's voice prompted.

I leaned back in my chair to look around Paisley. "Yeah?"

"I was just asking if your mom still has that rental," he clarified.

"Nope, Paisley's renting it."

Ward's gray eyes bounced from me to Paisley and back again, his brows hitching slightly. "Ah, so you're roommates."

Paisley interjected, "I wouldn't call us roommates. It's basically two separate apartments with a shared kitchen."

I didn't know why, but the fact she felt the need to make that point annoyed the hell out of me. "That's basically roommates," I added.

Ward looked from me to Paisley again, a grin teasing at the corners of his mouth. "Well then, I was just asking because Rowan's looking for a place."

I glanced over at Rowan. "I didn't know that."

"I'm set for the moment. Delilah and Alex are letting me rent the apartment above their garage, but I'd like a little more space eventually."

"It's hard to find rentals around here," Paisley commented. "Trust me, I looked for two months."

She practically vibrated with tension beside me, and I had to bite the insides of my cheeks to keep from saying something sarcastic. The conversation moved along with people chatting about town, about work, and so on. Meanwhile, I couldn't keep my focus off Paisley. I tried to ignore her, but it was nearly impossible with her sitting right beside me. At one point, she leaned over, and her arm brushed against mine. The subtle, barely-there touch felt like jagged electricity shooting up my arm. This was crazy. I reminded myself again and again about her point. It was *not* smart for me to want her. I shouldn't have kissed her. Not that it was entirely my fault. She was the one who got so close I couldn't resist. My critical mind rolled its eyes at that. Whatever. I would have to figure out how to deal.

All in all, it was a usual night with friends at the bar. We chatted about work, commiserated about a few things, and I noticed a distinction as the conversation carried on. Only me, Rowan, Chase, and Paisley weren't in committed relationships. Everyone else was settled down. Maybe they hadn't had kids yet, but they were on the way. I wasn't sure what I wanted from life, but I didn't know how much longer I wanted to keep things the way they were.

Yet, every time I thought about settling down, which my mom had been yammering at me about lately, I felt antsy. I knew what it was like to lose someone. Not because I'd been in love before, but because I'd responded to the call that ended with me finding my father dead. That had sent me spinning. My parents had been the real deal. They'd actually loved each other. My mom was still coming out of her grief, and I'd been devastated. It felt as if life had sideswiped me.

Sometimes, I wondered why I hadn't simply left town. The only reason I hadn't was the very reason I wanted to run: my father. He would've wanted me to be here for my mom but also to do right by my own life. He knew how much I loved firefighting, and that I had followed in his footsteps because of it. I couldn't let him down even though he wasn't here anymore.

Restless with my thoughts, I drained my beer and glanced around the table. "I'm gonna call it a night. Good to see everyone." I stood, waving at the chorus of goodbyes. I felt Paisley's eyes on me. Even though I knew it wasn't smart, I looked down and braced myself for that sizzle of electricity between us. The air crackled with it, and I felt the searing heat race through me. I turned away and strode outside quickly. As I drove home, I wondered how long she would stay out, then immediately berated myself for it.

## Chapter Twelve
# PAISLEY

My footsteps crunched on the gravel as I walked toward my car. It was parked at the edge of the parking lot, which ran parallel to the lake. I walked to the front of my car, stopping where the gravel met the grass. There was a frost tonight, and the grass crunched under my boots. I took a few steps farther and leaned my head back to look up at the stars glittering in the inky night. They felt so close here as if I could reach up and touch them.

My breath misted in the air, and I breathed in a deep gulp of the crisp late autumn air. Lowering my gaze, I looked out across the lake. The water rippled under the shimmer of light cast from the lodge behind me. There were houses scattered along the lake's shores, their lights peeking through the trees. I tried to place where Russell's house was, but I wasn't exactly sure.

Just thinking about the house sent a wash of heat through me and my thoughts spun to Russell. I just couldn't seem to turn off my attraction to him. It didn't matter that it wasn't sensible or that it annoyed the living hell out of me. I could only hope it would wear off soon. With one last look at the sky, I climbed in my car and drove home.

I turned the word "home" over in my thoughts. I didn't really know where my home was. Once upon a time, I'd loved the small town where I grew up in Washington. My hometown was in the foothills of the Cascade Mountains, beautiful and lush. My dad was the county district attorney and proud of his work, while my mother loved her florist business and puttered in greenhouses all year long. Growing up, my brother and I had been close even though he was two years older than me. Aside from the common complaints about his teasing and occasionally being obnoxious, he was a good brother.

At least, he *had* been. It wasn't that he was a bad brother now, but I was tired of keeping his secrets. Secrets I'd stumbled across by accident. Secrets that had driven me to live anywhere but my small hometown. It was true that I wanted to travel and see more of the world. I loved being a firefighter, and Alaska was a clarion call in the distance that drew me. It was also true that I'd been impatient to get out of town once I knew my brother's secrets and knew that he knew that I knew. Too much knowledge tangled up between us, and all of it was a secret from our parents.

I still wasn't exactly sure how my brother had ended up in his position. He'd partied hard in college, but I hadn't realized he'd started dealing designer drugs. He told me it was extremely lucrative, and he had a handle on it. He told me he wouldn't get in trouble. He swore up and down he wasn't using himself. Oddly, I believed that detail, if only because he was somehow managing to do that, while also working as an accountant. He was always on top of things, and I'd never once seen him anything other than stone cold sober.

As I drove toward the only place I could call home right now, I shook my head. He *thought* he had a handle on it, but he also felt the need to warn me about people. What the fuck? I'd found out about the whole mess by accident. When my brother was out of town, I'd gone to check on his cat. Some guys had shown up while I was there and conducted "business" while I hid in the bathroom.

Utterly confused, I'd gone to Ryder, and to his credit, he'd simply told me the truth. Of course, only a week later, I was having dinner with my parents, and my dad mentioned that his office was looking into a drug ring in the area. I'd felt sick to my stomach until I'd found this job and moved away.

So ... home. *That* wasn't home anymore, and I didn't imagine it would be anytime soon. This was home for now, but it was new. Now, I had a roommate—or rather, *not* a roommate—who I'd stupidly kissed. Just as I pulled in to park in front of the house, my phone rang.

I wasn't thinking and tapped the button on the dash to answer. "Hey, Paisley." Ryder's voice carried into my car. "How's it going?"

Obviously, my brother had found a way around the number block. "It's fine." My stomach tightened because my brother rarely called lately just to chat. "Do you have a new warning for me?" I asked, figuring we might as well get through the difficult part of this conversation.

"No, why would you assume that?"

I rolled my eyes. "Because that's your life these days."

My brother sighed. "Paisley, I'm sorry. I wish you

didn't even know about this. You don't need to worry. I was honestly just calling to let you know that I wanted to plan something for Mom and Dad's anniversary."

"Next month?"

"Yeah. It'll be their thirty-fifth anniversary. Do you want to come down for a visit?"

My chest felt tight, and tears stung the backs of my eyes. Visiting meant putting up a good front. "I'll have to see if I can travel for work," I said, which was true. I was pretty sure Graham would give me a few days off even though I was new.

"Think about it. Even if you can't travel, let's plan something together."

"Okay," I managed.

"Love you, Pais."

"I love you too."

The line went quiet, and I turned my car off, sitting there for a few minutes while the sounds of the engine cooling ticked around me. I felt spun tight inside, and I wanted to jump out of my own skin. Restless, I climbed out of the car quickly and walked inside, completely forgetting to be careful about encountering Russell. The door clicked shut behind me, and the archway into our shared kitchen was right in front of me.

Russell was standing in the kitchen with his back to me. Without a shirt. My mouth went dry.

He was reaching for something on the counter. I watched the flex of his muscles in his back. Dear God. He turned as I stood there, and I prayed my mouth snapped shut in time. I swallowed as heat spun like fiery pinwheels through my body. I blinked and couldn't seem to do anything other than remain frozen where I was.

Russell arched a brow, turning and resting his hips on the counter as he took a swallow from a bottle of beer. As I had at the bar, I tracked the motion of his throat. My eyes dipped when he lowered his hand, watching the subtle motion of the muscles in his forearm. Every inch of him was delectable. He had a dusting of hair on his chest. My eyes dropped lower, tracking the defined contours and noting a small scar along his ribs.

I snapped to attention when he asked, "Get a good enough look?"

Well, all that did was send a hot jolt of anger through me, the anger spinning into the desire nearly electrifying my body. Lifting my chin, I replied, "Maybe."

I was feeling contrary and unsettled about so many things that had nothing to do with Russell. His eyes skated over my face, dipping down. I was suddenly aware that my jacket hung open, and I was wearing a V-neck T-shirt and jeans with boots. Nothing special, practically a uniform for me. But my nipples tightened to an ache, and I knew they were probably visible pressing against the cotton. I could feel the blazing heat of his gaze moving over me.

He was provoking me, and I knew it, but I couldn't turn away. We were caught in this magnetic dance. His eyes made their way back to mine at a leisurely pace.

"Why did you leave early?" I asked, surprising myself with my question.

He held my gaze for a moment, something flickering in his eyes before he replied, "For no particular reason."

His reply annoyed me. I rolled my eyes. "Okay." I turned to walk away, and then I heard him moving. His footsteps were slow and deliberate behind me. As if he had a thread attached to me, I turned around again.

"Going to bed?" he asked.

The man moved like a cat, smooth and quiet. My mouth was still dry, and I swallowed. I was hot all over, my skin prickling with awareness. I was acutely aware of the slick arousal at my core. There was that low tug in my belly, my body reacting to his instinctively. The next thing I knew, he was *right* in front of me, and I was scrambling to think. But thinking at this moment was the equivalent of trying to start a car with a dead battery. It just didn't happen. Reason and rational thought didn't catch hold.

Instead, my senses were alive, busy absorbing the cacophony of sensation created by Russell being close to me without a shirt.

My nipples were so tight, they hurt. I could feel the fabric of my clothes on my skin, and I wanted to shake it off. The sensation was almost irritating.

"Can't stand being close?" he asked.

My one-word reply came out in a frayed breath. "What?"

"It's early," he added when he stopped, *way* too freaking close to me.

I'd never been so aware of space in my life. By my measure, he was maybe a foot away. The potency of his presence radiated to me. I could feel the heat, sense his strength. And that magnetic pull to him had me consciously keeping my feet planted where they were already.

"So what?" I countered.

I had to clench my hands into fists because I wanted to touch him so badly. He was close enough for me to catch his scent—musky, woodsy. I felt wild and primal as if I was chasing a scent to get closer. His skin was burnished bronze, and I wanted to trail my fingertips over the ridges of his abdomen. I wanted to drag my tongue along the side of his neck. I wanted to taste him as much as I wanted him. I knew what it felt like to be in his arms—knew the feel of his strength and power—and I wanted it fiercely. I wanted to drink it in, to forget everything.

I expected him to taunt me. When he didn't, that was almost worse for the state of my body. His eyes searched my face.

"What's wrong?" he asked.

His voice broke through the echoing beat of my heart pounding in my ears. "What do you mean?"

"You look upset. Are you okay?"

I *was* upset because calls from my brother tended to do that these days. I hated what I had lost because of my brother's choices. I was keeping secrets I didn't want to keep. I worried about him, and I was angry with him. Occasionally, I worried about myself, but that was last on the list. I usually pushed that far out of my mind because it wasn't worth it. I would take the risks to my own safety if only I had the power to change all the rest. I never talked about my brother with anyone because I couldn't.

But somehow, Russell's question and the concern evident in his eyes tapped into something in me. I heard myself answering, "Family stuff."

Maybe that wasn't exactly confiding, but it was more than I offered to anyone. I suddenly felt vulnerable. Anger followed swiftly, my defenses rising. On the heels of that, I felt even more desperate for him to hold me close.

He nodded slowly. "Understood. Family has a way of getting to us in ways that no one else can. I don't mean that in a bad way. It's just the truth."

My head bobbed up and down in agreement. I didn't notice when he lifted his hand, but the sensation sent filaments of fire through me when his fingertips brushed across my cheek. I didn't realize my hair had caught on my earring. He loosened it gently before saying, "There. It was tangled."

That subtle touch practically undid me. I realized then that there was one surefire way to forget all my worries. Russell could deliver an escape.

It was crazy and stupid, but maybe it would be worth it because I wanted to forget so desperately. I needed to be delivered from the restless ache of needing him. Maybe diving into this was the only way out.

My feet moved closer. There were now maybe three inches separating us. Russell's eyes blinked as he looked down at me.

"It's not fair," I murmured.

His lips curled in a grin, slow and sensual. "What's not fair?"

My belly was tingling and spun in flips as liquid need spread like wildfire through my veins. "Your eyelashes. They're curly and thick." It was nothing but the truth.

He chuckled. "I've never paid attention to them."

"Well, you wouldn't," I retorted, a prick of annoyance following.

"What are you doing?" he asked, his eyes searching mine.

"Being reckless," I replied, more honestly than was probably smart.

He cocked his head to the side, a glint entering his eyes. "What's reckless?"

Reality slapped me. Because I knew Russell was dangerous to me somehow or, rather, to my sanity, I stepped back abruptly. "Never mind." I turned and started to make my way out of the kitchen when his voice caught me like a hook.

"What are you afraid of, Paisley?"

I spun back to face him, fury rising inside. My emotions were a jumble, and I wasn't thinking rationally. I was feeling too vulnerable.

"I'm not afraid of anything," I insisted when I stepped back toward him.

I didn't know who kissed who first. But the next thing I knew, I was held fast against him, his lips were angling over mine, and I was moaning into our kiss. His chest was everything—the muscled surface firm and his skin warm. His mouth was magic. This kiss went from zero to one hundred within the lick of a flame. His tongue swept into my mouth, and I was on my tippy toes as he held me against him. One of my hands clutched a muscled shoulder as the other slid around his neck, and I held on tight.

Our kiss felt like a war. My annoyance at my fierce need for him only drove my frustration higher. My reckless, unsettled state had me feeling feverish. Russell kissed just as good as I remembered with deep sweeps of his tongue followed by him gentling before nipping at my lips and diving back in. I had no idea how long we stood there, but somewhere along the way, he spun us around and pressed my back against the wall, which was absolutely perfect. I could brace against it as I curled my legs around his hips and whimpered at the feel of his arousal pressing between my thighs.

He shoved my coat off my shoulders, and I tore my arms loose from the sleeves, gasping when I felt his palm slide under my T-shirt. His touch was hot, a brand on my skin, and I trembled all over. His calloused palm coasted over the curve of my belly, and he cupped a breast. My nipple was so tight I cried out when his thumb brushed over it. Every nerve ending felt raw with almost unbearable sensitivity.

I had no idea how long we kissed until he broke free, and the sound of our ragged breathing ricocheted in the space. I was on fire, so needy. I lost all shame. I didn't care that I was annoyed with him or that this was stupid. I needed him, and I needed *only* him. An orgasm with my favorite vibrator would not do the trick tonight.

"Paisley." His gruff whisper had me lifting my heavy lids to stare into his eyes, dark with desire. "I thought you said this was stupid."

"It is," I whispered between ragged pants. "I still want you."

He closed his eyes, his brow creasing as he took a shuddering breath before his gaze met mine again. "We work together, and we live together."

"I don't care." My caution had been incinerated in the fire of his kiss.

We stared at each other, and I could feel the rapid beat of his heart under my palm, which had landed on his chest somewhere along the way.

"Your room or mine?" he asked after a long moment.

I hadn't seen his room, and I was curious. "Yours."

Russell never even put me down, which was *so* fucking sexy. He held me easily as he walked us down the stairs. I felt the friction of his hard arousal at the apex of my thighs with every step. The subtle motion nearly brought me to climax. I dipped my head and dragged my tongue along his collarbone, savoring the salty tang of his skin.

"Wait," he murmured. "You're going to drive me crazy, Paisley."

I loved how he made me feel alive and wild. And, as if maybe, just maybe, this wasn't only me. A moment later, we were walking into his space. He nudged the light on with his elbow. It was basically a replica of my place. I barely had time to absorb any details before he kicked open the door to his bedroom. With another nudge of his elbow, a lamp came on in the corner.

My eyes snagged on the navy-blue down quilt, and then Russell was lowering me to the bed. In one smooth move, his hand hooked the hem of my T-shirt and tossed it aside. He let out a rough groan and cupped my breasts, dipping his head and dropping hot kisses in the valley between them. Cool air struck my skin as he flicked the clasp on my bra. With a shimmy, I slipped the straps free of my arms, and my bra was tossed to the floor.

I cried out at the feel of his warm mouth closing over a nipple and giving it a sharp suck. Each sensation collided with the next. My senses were scrambled with pleasure. He murmured hot words, dirty words, telling me I was beautiful, sexy, and so fucking hot.

"Boots gotta go," he said, lifting his head before straightening and stepping back.

He shoved down the sweatpants he was wearing. My core clenched tight at the sight of him in fitted black briefs with his thick cock outlined. Staring at Russell was almost more than I could take. He cleared his throat.

"Oh." I hurriedly shimmied to the edge of the bed and kicked off my boots.

He was ever helpful, unbuttoning my jeans and shoving them down. In a hot second, I was lifted in the air, landing on the bed as he came down beside me. I stared up at him, trying to catch my breath, trying to think. His eyes coasted over me. His gaze was burning, leaving sparks in its wake on my skin.

"I knew you were dangerous," he murmured, his voice low and gravelly.

"Dangerous?"

His eyes met mine as he nodded slowly.

## Chapter Thirteen
# RUSSELL

Paisley's jade eyes blinked up at me. Her cheeks were flushed, and her lips were kiss bitten. She was fucking dangerous. Jesus. Her breasts were round, just enough to fill my palms. Her nipples were dusky pink and taut. I couldn't help it and dipped my head again to swirl my tongue around one and give it a suck. I savored the way she trembled underneath me and let out a sharp cry.

"Russell," she murmured.

I lifted my head. "Yes?"

"What do you mean I'm dangerous?" she pressed.

"You're so hot, and well, you're dangerous for me because I can't think."

I slid my palm over her belly. Her skin was warm and dewy. I brought my lips to her skin again, this time following the random scatter of freckles on one side of her belly. She was wearing practical black cotton panties, which suited her. I let my hand slide down between her thighs, teasing over the damp cotton. I doubted she was as turned on as me because that would be fucking impossible.

I was so hard I was riding the edge of pain. I'd kept my briefs on for a reason. I knew the minute I was naked I'd need to be inside her. I wanted this to be good for Paisley and didn't want to rush through it. Her hips rocked into my hand, and she let out something between a moan and a whimper. I only had so much restraint and hooked a finger over the edge of the elastic, tugging her panties down over her hips. She was helpful, lifting her hips and shimmying as she kicked her panties free from her ankles.

My gaze landed on the tidy thatch of auburn hair, and I sifted my fingers through her curls and dipped into her folds. My fingers became instantly slick with her arousal, and she impatiently bucked into my touch, her pussy clenching around me as I delved into her.

Paisley could be so cranky with me and so quick to argue. Fuck, I loved how fiery she was. I also loved that she was wet—*for me*.

She gasped my name. I lifted my head. "Yes?"

I sank two fingers in her, and her eyes fell closed as she arched back. Fuck me. I wanted all of it at once. I wanted to tease her breasts and taste every inch of her skin, but I was busy fucking her with my fingers.

I pressed hot, open-mouthed kisses on her belly while she shuddered underneath me. Shifting lower, I pushed her thighs apart and finally tasted her. She was salty and sweet, her scent musky. I licked into her folds, loving her incoherent cries and her impatience with me. Her orgasm came faster than I expected when I swirled my tongue around her clit, and she tensed before her entire body trembled when she let out a sharp, keening cry.

My mind was hazed with need. I rose, rolling to the side and fumbling for a condom in my night table.

I shucked my briefs when I stood. When I lifted my gaze, I found Paisley's eyes opened wide.

"Come here," she murmured as she propped herself up on an elbow.

I still had the condom in my hand, but I stepped close to her. My knees sank into the mattress when she curled her palm around my throbbing length. Her thumb swiped over the bead of cum rolling out. With her eyes on mine, she licked her thumb clean.

"That is the sexiest thing I've ever seen," I growled.

She leaned forward to swirl her tongue around the tip of my cock, then she sucked me in quick. I almost came right then and was relieved when she drew back.

"I need to be inside you," I said flatly.

She shimmied back on the bed as I swiftly rolled the condom down my length. Seconds later, I was resting in the cradle of her hips, and her legs were curling around me. I filled her in a swift surge.

She let out a ragged breath. My speech was slurred as my forehead fell to hers. "Fuck, you feel so good."

She moaned in response, wiggling her hips slightly as I seated myself fully. I held still for a beat because I knew I didn't have much time left before I came. My balls were drawing up tight, and I could feel the hot sizzle at the base of my spine. Resting on an elbow, I drew back and thrust inside her deeply. Reaching between us, I teased my fingers over her slippery and swollen clit. She was already clenching around me and sounded startled.

"Oh! Oh, my god."

Then, she was shuddering with another cry, and I followed her over. My release whipped through me. My mind went blank as white-hot electricity vibrated through me. I fell to the side, rolling her with me.

I'd known I wanted Paisley, and it would be good with us, but desire was fickle. Sometimes what you thought would be good wasn't good after all, but that wasn't the case with Paisley. She was like her own magic elixir.

She fell against me warm and soft, her skin damp. I lay there stunned, trying to absorb the implications of just how amazing that was. After a moment, I felt her eyes on me and dragged mine open. She looked as startled as I felt.

She took a shuddery breath. "It wasn't supposed to be that good," she said bluntly.

A tiny voice in the back of my mind tried to tell me I should disengage, and she should go upstairs. We should keep this contained, stuff this magic back into a bottle and cork it. But I didn't feel like listening to that voice right then.

Paisley was soft, she was warm, and I didn't want her to leave. I slid my hand up and down her back. After a few minutes, she shifted, and I slipped out of her. I rolled away and walked into the bathroom to deal with the condom. I thought maybe she would have more sense than me and leave. But a moment later, after I'd washed my hands and splashed cold water on my face, I returned to the bedroom to find her still lying there, curled on her side.

When I reached the bed again, I lifted the covers, and she blinked up at me. "You're getting cold," I pointed out.

I knew this because I could see the goose bumps on her skin. She shimmied and rolled under the covers with me. I fell asleep with her held close, not even letting myself think about how crazy and stupid this was.

## Chapter Fourteen
# PAISLEY

The following morning, I stood under the hot water as it beat down on me. My body was still pinging with desire and the sated aftermath of yet another orgasm delivered by Russell's nimble fingers. He left me relaxed and boneless in a way I had never been before. I should've been freaking out, but I couldn't even bring myself to do it.

He'd already left the house, and this morning should've been awkward, but somehow, it wasn't. I knew we would argue again. I knew it would get weird, but I wanted to relax in this bubble for now. I'd woken to his warm hands teasing me awake. We'd fallen into slow, teasing kisses. He'd deftly rolled a condom on before sliding into me from behind. He slowly brought me to an orgasm that rolled in deep waves through me, sending shudders all the way to my toes.

After that, he'd made pancakes, which were very good. He'd finally left to go help his mom with something. I knew the regret would come, but at this moment, my body felt as if I had been someone else's sensual feast, and I wanted to savor the feeling.

I didn't have to work today, so I wondered what I should do with myself. After getting dressed with my skin still feeling hypersensitive, I was relieved when my phone rang, and Phoebe asked if I wanted to meet her for coffee. That was perfect. A little distraction would help.

Once we were seated at a table at Firehouse Café, Phoebe looked over at me, commenting, "Well, you look like someone who had a *very* good night."

"Um, what?"

Her lips twitched. "You don't need to tell me anything, but there's a vibe."

"Oh, my God." I looked over at Phoebe, feeling the heat flash into my cheeks. Not for the first time, I wished I didn't blush so easily. Auburn hair came with fair skin and freckles and blushes, at least in my case. "What do you mean?" I countered, trying to sound nonchalant and probably failing.

Her brows hitched up, and she smiled slightly before shrugging. "Nothing, I guess."

I cleared my throat and took a swallow of my coffee. "Just had a good night's sleep."

"That's always a win," she replied easily.

I was relieved when she dropped it at that. We chatted about work as we sipped our coffee. I looked toward the door when I heard someone call Phoebe's name. Glancing over, I saw Madison Glen waving over at our table. She was with Graham, my new boss, the very guy who'd picked up on the tension between Russell and me and told us to stop arguing. He'd even forced us to talk about it.

Even though there was *no* way Graham could've known what happened last night, I suddenly felt guilty. Madison was stunning. Her almost black hair hung in a glossy fall down her back. She wore fitted jeans tucked into cowboy boots and a belted sweater under a lightweight down jacket. She even looked good in a cute knitted hat. I could *never* pull off a look like that.

Phoebe smiled over at her. "Hey, Madison."

Madison turned and said something to Graham, and he released her hand as he leaned over and pressed a kiss to her cheek. The only word to describe the look he gave her was hot.

"Wow, Graham's got it bad," I commented to Phoebe.

Her eyes twinkled with her smile. "He sure does."

Madison stopped by the table, dividing her gaze between us. "How's it going?" she asked.

Phoebe nodded and gestured to me. "Good. You two have met, right?"

Madison looked down at me with a warm smile. "We have, but only for a minute. You're on Graham's crew, right?"

"I am."

"I've been in town a few weeks longer than you," she offered with a wink. She slipped her cream-colored knit hat off, smoothing a hand over her hair. "I just moved here a few months ago, and I'm still getting adjusted. Moving somewhere new can be a little intimidating. I'm guessing you're handling it better than me because you're a firefighter."

The uncertainty that flickered in her eyes relaxed me. While she was gorgeous, her openness about the travails of moving somewhere new mirrored my own insecurities. "I don't know about that. I can handle a fire, but moving is always a challenge."

"I'm a city girl, and it's easier to be invisible in the city. I like this small town, but it's different," she observed. "Where are you from?"

"A small town in Washington, just outside the Cascades."

"So, you know the small town drill, then?" Her lips quirked with her question.

I shrugged. "Sort of. I have learned that rentals are hard to come by here."

Madison chuckled. "Now, I lucked out there. I inherited my grandfather's place. That's what brought me here."

"You want to sit with us?" Phoebe asked.

Madison glanced over her shoulder toward Graham, who was now at the front of the line, then looked back at Phoebe. "Sure. Graham and I drove here in separate cars because he's headed into the station after this."

She sat down in one of the empty chairs across from me. "So, did you know Graham before you moved here?" I asked.

Her hair swung on her shoulders when she shook her head. "I didn't know anyone. It's a new relationship." A tinge of pink crested on her cheeks.

"He's a good boss," I offered.

"And a really nice guy," Phoebe added.

"You've known him for a long time because you grew up here, right?" Madison prompted when she looked toward Phoebe.

Phoebe nodded. "That's right. Graham's always been a good guy. He grew up fast when he had Allie."

I'd heard Graham was a single father, but it still surprised me. "How old is his daughter?" I interjected.

Madison's lips twitched at the corners. "She's a freshman in high school, just turned fourteen. She's a good kid, but she's definitely been testing him lately."

At that moment, Graham arrived beside our table,

immediately handing Madison a coffee cup and a plate with a bagel on it.

"The bagels here are really good," I commented.

"I know. I was so relieved when I got a job because then I didn't have to worry about cutting back on my coffee time and bagels here," she said with a little laugh.

Graham chuckled, dipping his head in acknowledgment to Phoebe and me. "I'm headed to the station. Will I see you two there?"

Phoebe cocked her head to the side. "Noooo," she said slowly. "Our crew isn't on duty this weekend. Why are you going in?"

Madison's laughter rang out, and she looked up at him. "He's a workaholic."

Graham shifted on his feet, looking sheepish. "I'm just doing a little paperwork, that's all. I'm only working half the day." I was relieved at his explanation. He didn't seem like the kind of boss who expected us to be working when we weren't on duty, but I was still new enough that I wasn't totally sure. "I'd better get going. I'll see you tonight." When he looked down at Madison, the intimacy flickering in his eyes made my heart squeeze, and I felt as if I should look away.

Madison blinked up at him, reaching for his hand and giving it a little tug. He leaned down and dropped a lingering kiss on her lips before straightening. "Yes, you'll see me later." She waved with her fingers, her nails perfectly done, of course, as he left.

Phoebe cast Madison a sideways look. "That man has got it bad for you."

Madison flushed, shrugging. "I'm not so sure."

"Uh, I may not know you well, but I have to agree with Phoebe on that," I offered dryly.

Madison took a deep breath and a sip of her coffee.

"Maybe he does, but I'm not used to it." After another sip of coffee, she divided her gaze between us. "What are you two up to today?"

"Meeting for coffee," Phoebe replied with a laugh.

"Well, I'm headed to Anchorage for some errands. Want to keep me company?" Madison asked.

As soon as she looked at us, uncertainty flickered in her eyes, and she began to open her mouth again before Phoebe interjected quickly. "Of course! Can we go to Costco?"

"Oh, there's a Costco in Anchorage?" I cut in.

Phoebe nodded firmly. "There are two."

"Well, count me in."

"We can do whatever you want. I just need to drop some paperwork off at the office. I'm also trying to make friends. In order to do that, I've been told I actually have to reach out to people," Madison explained.

Phoebe gave her an understanding look. "It's hard to make friends when you're a grown-up."

Since we were on the topic, I nodded in agreement. "It's weird."

"Well, we have a shopping trip," Madison said. "Plus, I want to hear about Russell."

The minute Madison said that, I felt a blush creeping up my cheeks. "What do you mean?" I ground out.

"Graham thinks Russell likes you, and now you're roommates."

I closed my eyes and let out a sigh. I wasn't going to fess up about last night because *that* would be a problem. Opening them, I tried to shrug casually. "I have no idea what Russell thinks or if he likes me. Plus, we're not really roommates."

"What do you mean?" Phoebe asked.

"I rent the upstairs, and he's downstairs. It's kind of like two separate apartments, but in the same house."

Madison's lips twitched, and there was a mischievous glint in her eyes. Phoebe was responding to a text on her phone while Madison took a bite of her bagel. When she finished chewing, she offered, "Sure, you're not roommates then. Whatever makes it easier for you."

Phoebe set her phone down, chiming in with, "I can't speak for Russell, but I think you have a crush on him."

## Chapter Fifteen
# PAISLEY

The weekend passed, and by some miracle, Russell and I managed to politely avoid each other at the house. I couldn't say it was entirely on purpose, but it worked out that way. It was fine because I needed it to be that way. I wasn't ready to face him, not after what had transpired between us. I needed a little space to gather my composure and avoid doing something completely stupid.

Monday rolled around, and I went to work. Everything was fine. Fine, meaning that Russell and I managed to make eye contact, and I didn't combust on the spot. Fine, meaning that we did a training exercise and even handled a nearby call. Everything was fine. We weren't arguing. However, I was tense, like seriously tense, but I managed. Fortunately, with twenty-five people on our crew, I didn't have to be close to Russell at all times.

He seemed to have put a moratorium on teasing me. I wanted him to tease me, and I missed it, and I hated that I missed it. He was a magnet, and I was steel, like that song. I kept looking at him again and again and again, and then yanking my eyes away. It was beyond annoying.

Adding to my frustration, he seemed more successful at *not* looking at me. Or at least that was how it felt. One day after we returned to the station, I showered in the small locker area for the women and changed. When I walked through the reception area, I saw Maisie chatting with Madison, who saw me immediately and waved. "Hey!"

Madison looked amazing with her hair up in a twist and a soft-looking sweater outlining her curves. She looked at Maisie. "We went to Anchorage together. I'm making friends."

I angled over, smiling when I stopped at the circular desk where Maisie sat. "We went to Costco together. I think that's a true bonding experience," I offered.

Maisie smiled at us. "I love Costco."

"Who doesn't love Costco? It's the best," Madison insisted firmly. "When I moved up here from Houston, I was concerned I'd feel like I was in the middle of nowhere. Not that I like to shop all that much, but a good grocery store is important. The local one here is decent, but Anchorage is not even an hour away."

Maisie paused to take a call as I asked, "Do you miss the city?"

Madison shrugged. "Not really. Houston was all I knew before I moved up here, but honestly, I like it here more. We'll see how I feel after winter, though. It's starting to get cold."

Maisie ended her call, catching the tail end of Madison's comment. "You'll be able to handle winter, I promise. I moved up here from California. Maybe that's not as hot as Texas, but you get used to the weather. You've got a nice jacket, so you should be set." She gestured to Madison's fluffy down jacket.

Madison smiled. "Graham teases me. I might have overdone it with the online shopping for winter. I have three down coats. He says it's not as cold as I think."

Maisie laughed. "It's not so bad. This part of Alaska isn't like up north, where it's dark and below zero for months. It's not dark all winter here."

"Is that a myth?" Madison asked.

Maisie rolled her eyes. "Not entirely. The days *are* shorter, but the sun only goes away completely up north. Here, the sun comes up around nine and sets around four."

The door to the back hallway opened, and Russell and Graham came walking through. Graham stopped at Madison's side, sliding his arm around her waist. "Hey there. Give me ten minutes, and I'll be ready."

"Ten whole minutes?" she teased.

Graham arched a brow. "Yes, you're early." He glanced at his watch.

"I'll chat with the girls. It's no big deal," she offered with a slow smile.

My eyes, because of that whole magnet issue, were drawn to Russell. For the first time in days, I caught him looking at me. It felt as if an electrical line sparked in the air between us. I immediately looked away, my gaze landing on Maisie, who gave me a knowing look. A moment later, Graham and Russell had disappeared through the opposite doorway into the police station side of the building.

Maisie looked from me to Madison, just as Madison said, "Wow, that was a look."

I stayed quiet while my cheeks flamed. Maisie chimed in with, "Agreed."

Now I couldn't help myself. "What are you talking about?"

"The way Russell looked at you, and the way you looked at him," Madison pointed out.

I sighed. "There was no look. There's no *there* there."

"If you say so," Maisie sing-songed.

I was relieved when a call came in for Maisie, and our conversation was cut short.

## Chapter Sixteen
# RUSSELL

A full week passed where Paisley and I did a dance of calculated avoidance. While I couldn't say for sure it was calculated on her part, it certainly was on mine. The most interaction we had was at work, and every encounter, no matter how brief, had a thread of fiery tension running through it. I didn't even know what to do with how good it had been with her. It was honestly the single best night I'd ever had.

It burned like a flare in the sky. The recollection of sensations flamed hot every time I saw her. It took an effort to keep my focus on work. I managed, somehow, to avoid being alone with her at the house. I was a busy guy. I'd always been a busy guy, so I found one convenient excuse after another to be occupied.

It rankled that we shared the same work schedule. I'd shifted from being annoyed about my attraction to her to being annoyed that I'd given in to it. I wanted nothing more than *more* with her, but tumbling into bed with her again wouldn't be smart.

I knew how insanely good it felt to be with her. I knew how silky smooth her skin was. I knew she had freckles scattered like constellations on her body. I knew the way the weight of her breast felt in my palm and how her nipple ruched tightly under the brush of my thumb. I knew she tasted sweet and musky. I knew she was warm. And I knew what it felt like to come inside her when she trembled beneath me.

None of that mattered, yet it *all* mattered. At some point, I wouldn't be able to keep avoiding her all the time. We lived in the same house, for fuck's sake. Even though she wanted to dispute the technicalities of it, we were roommates.

I rested my palms against the tiled wall of the shower one morning, letting my head hang down as the hot water pounded between my shoulder blades. The heat eased the soreness there. I'd been going in early and working out at the station, pushing myself to the limit. Graham even commented on it, but I'd just told him I wanted to get in better shape. That seemed like something a guy could say, especially when said guy's job required being intensely fit at all times. He'd accepted my explanation, but not without first giving me a searching look. As luck would have it, his new girlfriend, Madison, showed up and distracted him.

I was happy for Graham. He'd been raising his daughter on his own for years. He was a solid friend and a good guy who deserved to find love. I couldn't help but chuckle as I straightened. He still seemed surprised by Madison. While there wasn't a single spark for me with her, I wasn't blind. She was a stunner. It was good to see them together. Of course, thinking about that had me thinking about my mother's conversation with me the other night.

For fuck's sake, she could *not* let it go. She felt like I should be in a relationship by now. My father's death had hit us both hard. I still missed him and knew I would for the rest of my life. Just thinking about him now caused my heart to give an achy thump. My mom had gotten past the initial shock of her grief. For reasons I didn't understand, she was now focused on making sure I found someone to love. She kept saying she didn't want me to miss having what she and my dad had.

I groaned. I was in a muddle. Between my mom not shutting up about love and that fiery night with Paisley, nothing felt clear anymore. I'd honestly believed I could keep things casual. When Paisley said we had to keep it that way, I thought that was smart. I just hadn't fully comprehended the effect she would have on me.

Although I was studiously avoiding her, it rankled that she was doing the same in return. I couldn't tell if that meant she wasn't as affected by me as I was her or something else. I gave my head a shake and looked down. I wasn't even thinking about her in a sexual way, and my cock was swelling at the mere thought of her.

I did what I'd been doing almost daily since our night together and went for a quick release in the shower. It wasn't even that satisfying, but it took the edge off my need for her.

After getting dressed, I went upstairs, assuming she wouldn't be around, and was surprised to find her in the kitchen. She was wearing a loose T-shirt and a pair of leggings. I wanted to yank all of her clothes off, bend her over the counter, and fuck her right here in the kitchen. My cock twitched again, and I kicked those thoughts to the curb. She spun around quickly, her eyes widening when she saw me.

"Morning, Paisley," I said, dipping my chin slightly as I walked past her.

I started the coffeemaker, and I sensed her

leaving the room. My hackles rose, and I turned. "Are you seriously not going to say anything?" I called.

She stopped in the archway, and I saw the set of her shoulders stiffen. Turning to face me, she narrowed her eyes. "Good morning, Russell," she said politely.

Her tone was crisp and stilted. Without another word, she turned and walked away. I didn't miss the pink flush staining her cheeks. I had to clench my hands into fists to keep from following her. Snagging a container of yogurt out of the fridge, I devoured it. While I waited for the coffee to finish, the house phone rang again, the sound jarring in the room.

Curious, I crossed over and answered it. "Hello."

"Hi there, I'm looking for Paisley," a man said.

"Sure. Can I ask who's calling?"

"It's her brother."

"Okay, give me a second. She's upstairs."

Setting the phone on the counter and chuckling as I looked at the long cord, I turned and jogged up the stairs. Paisley had closed her door.

I knocked, calling out, "Paisley, you've got a phone call."

I could've just turned and gone back downstairs. Instead, I waited—because I craved being close to her. It wasn't as if I expected to act on my urges, but I wanted to be near her. I wanted to absorb the feel of her presence, even if it was her prickly attitude. I wanted to watch her eyes and the way they darkened.

A full minute passed as I waited. After a glance at my watch, I knocked again. "Paisley?"

She opened the door, a crease forming between her brows. "What's up?"

"You have a phone call."

A stillness settled in her expression. "Okay," she finally said. "On the house phone?"

"Yeah, it's your brother."

For a split second, I could've sworn I saw fear in her eyes, followed immediately by sadness and then irritation. Brushing past me, she jogged down the stairs while I followed. My eyes lingered on the lush curve of her bottom.

A moment later, she picked up the phone in the kitchen. "Hey," she said curtly.

I couldn't hear what her brother said, but she nodded along before saying, "I haven't said anything to Mom and Dad. I told you that."

My curiosity was piqued, but I kept my back to her while I got my coffee ready. She didn't need to know just how curious I was. Something felt off about her brother. A moment later, she hung up the phone. I glanced over my shoulder to see her hand still curled around the phone receiver, her knuckles almost white. Her other hand was curled into a fist at her side. Her cheeks had two bright pink spots just under her eyes. She looked upset and shaken.

I acted on reflex. "Are you okay?" I crossed over to her.

Her gaze bounced to me before darting away. She uncurled her hand from the receiver and set it in the cradle before shrugging. "I'm fine." Her tone was flat, and it was obvious she was anything but fine.

"Hey," I said, resting my hands on her shoulders. "You don't look fine. What's wrong?"

When she looked up at me, I could see her almost warring with herself before she let out a deep sigh. A tear rolled down her cheek. Aw, hell. I didn't handle crying well. I didn't know what to do, so I simply folded my arms around her.

"I don't know what's going on, but it'll be okay."

I could feel a subtle tremor running through her, and I was startled at the deep protectiveness that coursed through me. I didn't know what was going on with her brother, but whatever she was upset about had something to do with him, and I didn't like it.

I held her carefully, sliding one palm up and down her back in soothing passes. "It'll be okay," I repeated.

She shook her head against my chest, mumbling, "No, I don't think it will."

I took a step back, sliding my hands down her arms before releasing one and lifting her chin with a slight nudge of my knuckles. "What's wrong? Can I help?"

She blinked, her eyes intensely green. Her lashes were spiky from the tears she wiped away with a palm. She shrugged again. "I appreciate you asking, but I don't think so. My brother's an idiot."

"Is he?" I heard myself asking. "It can't be all that bad."

She swallowed audibly. "It's a mess is what it is, and I don't know how to fix it."

"Do you want to talk about it?"

She shook her head. I glanced at the clock on the wall above the phone. "Well, what are you planning to do today?"

She shrugged. "I didn't have any plans."

"Let's go for a hike."

Her brows hitched up, her eyes widening. "A hike?"

"Yeah, a hike."

"You and me?" she prompted.

My lips tugged into a smile. "Yes, you and me, go for a hike. Or I don't know, whatever you want to do." I wanted to take her mind off her brother and whatever the hell was going on with him. "We could go to the beach. Have you been there yet?" She shook her head. "Let's go then. I'll drive you down to one of my favorite spots." She was still eyeing me curiously like she wasn't sure. "Maybe I can't help you with your brother, or maybe you don't want me to help you, but a little distraction can't hurt. Especially when you're feeling helpless about something."

Paisley smiled slowly, and it felt like a banner unfurling across my heart. I *really* wanted her to smile. I wanted to chase away whatever was worrying her. I didn't even want to think too much about how important it was for me that she felt okay.

## Chapter Seventeen
# RUSSELL

I should have thought this through. Driving in my truck with Paisley made me acutely aware of the space inside my truck cab more than anything *ever* had. She was right *here*. I could reach across the console and touch her if I wanted. Her scent drifted around me, and she smelled a little sweet. She was looking out the window as I drove, and I caught myself sneaking glances of her—again and again and again. I loved the lines of her profile, the sweep of her cheekbone, and the way her nose tipped up at the end.

My eyes tracked the smattering of freckles on her cheeks, looking like gold dust in the filtered sunlight cast through the window. She turned, almost catching me looking at her.

"Can I roll the window down?"

I glanced her way again. "Sure, but it's a little chilly out."

"I don't mind. I love the smell of the ocean."

I felt my lips tugging into a smile. "Go for it. If you get cold, we'll just blast the heat."

Paisley laughed, and I was glad to see her relaxing.

I couldn't help but worry about whatever the hell was going on with her brother, but I kicked those worries away for now. This was the second time he'd called the house phone, which, in all honesty, was odd. That house phone was there only because my parents had put it there years back when they built the place. That was well before cell phones were commonly used.

The house had been modernized, but we still had that phone line. As my dad pointed out the year before he passed away, cell reception was sometimes questionable. It was just strange that her brother didn't call her cell phone. Even my mom rarely called that landline when she called me.

Autumn air swirled into the truck when Paisley cracked her window. The air was bracing and cool, but I didn't mind. I loved the smell of fall. The air was crisp, carrying the scents of evergreen, hints of woodsmoke, and the rich, earthy feel of everything falling back to the ground to be covered up by the snow.

"Oh, I can see the ocean!" Paisley was pointing in the distance, where Cook Inlet was visible through the trees.

I smiled over at her. "Give it a few, and you'll have a better view."

Only moments later, we rounded a curve in the highway cresting the top of a hill. The view of the inlet spilled out in front of us. Alaska was abundant with its natural beauty. Growing up here, I felt spoiled sometimes. I'd never tired of it, and I'd even missed it while I was gone in college. The jagged peaks of a mountain range in the distance were dark against the skyline, and the sunlight glittered on the water like hard diamonds.

"Where are we going?" Paisley rolled up her

window, the last word of her question loud once the wind stopped.

"There's a viewing area where we can park and walk along the beach."

She actually bounced in her seat. "Really?"

"That's what I said." I chuckled, adding, "You rolled up the window."

She shrugged. "It is chilly. I'm glad I wore my jacket and my boots." She bounced her heels on the floor. She was short, her feet barely reaching the floorboard in my truck.

Of course, because my mind had a problem when it came to Paisley, that thought was followed by the memory of how she fit perfectly against me. My body recalled the visceral feel of her legs curled around my hips. I mentally groaned. Fuck me. I needed to get a handle on this.

I kept my eyes on the road and was relieved Paisley seemed content to look out the window. A few minutes later, I slowed down and turned off the highway. We drove down a narrow gravel road through a cluster of trees that opened up to a clearing and a rocky beach.

Paisley practically leaped out once I parked. I turned off the engine and pocketed my keys, making sure to lock my truck. Crime was low in Alaska, but parking in secluded areas sometimes led to people helping themselves if the opportunity offered itself.

I followed Paisley as she hurried down a slope to the rocky beach. She stopped, lifting her head and glancing around. "It's so beautiful." Her eyes were wide when she looked over at me. "Does it ever get old?"

An eagle screeched in the air, and she looked away, her eyes scanning the area. I pointed down the beach.

"See that outcropping of trees on the bluff? They usually nest right there."

An eagle proved me right by flying out of the trees and screeching again as if it had heard me. "It never gets old."

"Wow." Paisley's tone was reverential as she watched the massive bird take flight. "I've seen plenty of eagles in Willow Brook, but I'm still shocked by how big they are."

I chuckled. "Have you been to the town transfer station yet?"

Her head whipped my way, questions swirling in her eyes. "The transfer station?"

"Yeah, it's the best place to see them. It's open tomorrow. You can go with me. I need to swing by anyway."

She blinked at me. "Are you serious?"

"Absolutely. They're scavenger birds and not picky, so the transfer station offers them easy dining. They also love to hang around the cleaning stations near the fishing areas and docks."

"Cleaning stations?"

"Tables where people fillet the fish they catch."

Paisley laughed. "Eagles are so majestic, but that makes them sound lazy."

I shrugged. "They're smart and opportunistic. No sense in making more work when it's not necessary." I gestured for her to follow me. "Come on, let's walk."

We meandered along the shoreline, and I promptly discovered she loved rocks. Alaska's beaches had excellent rocks. While the gray rocks dominated, they were mingled with colors—red, green, purple, pink, orange, and the occasional lava that had fallen in the ocean and formed into almost weightless shapes. Paisley filled her pockets and then mine.

The sun was giving its bow in the sky when I glanced over at Paisley. "We should probably head back." I looked at my watch. "I want to get back to the truck before it gets dark. We're pretty safe here, but we *are* in bear country, and moose are always nearby."

Paisley's eyes widened, and she immediately turned, picking up her pace as we began to walk back toward the parking area. When I heard a splashing sound, I glanced over to see a seal rising out of the water. I tapped Paisley on the shoulder, pointing toward the seal.

She clapped her hand to her mouth. "Oh, my god! It's a seal. They're so cute." Her eyes glittered with excitement when she looked back at me, and my heart twisted sharply in my chest.

Not only had that night with her been the hottest night in my life but she also got to me. My reaction to her had shifted from one of irritation and lust to like, and perhaps more than lust. I danced away from those thoughts like a horse shying when startled.

"Cute, aren't they? They're also curious. I wouldn't be surprised if this one follows us all the way back to the parking area."

Her brows hitched up in question as she cast me a doubtful look.

"You watch."

Just as the eagle had earlier, the seal proved me right. It dived under the water and repeatedly surfaced again as we walked, always glancing over as if to check on what we were doing. We reached the parking area just as the sun touched the top of a mountain range in the distance. The bright orange ball in the sky left a wake of colors swirling behind it. An owl called nearby, and I breathed in the crisp ocean air before glancing down at Paisley.

Her green eyes blinked as she looked up at me, and it felt as if she sent a dart to the corner of my heart. The need to kiss her slammed into me so fiercely it stole my breath.

## Chapter Eighteen
# PAISLEY

Russell stared down at me, his eyes darkening. With the light fading as dusk took hold, I felt caught in the beam of his gaze. I could hear the vroom of my pulse picking up speed. My breath was shallow as heat bloomed through me in a wash, sending goose bumps prickling over the surface of my skin.

An owl called in the distance again, a magpie chattering in return. The two birds' activity intersected at this between time of twilight. The sky swirled with the sounds of nature around us—the slow rhythm of the tide going out, a quiet splash in the water, the subtle sound of a chilly gust of air, and another call from an owl. I felt pulled, all of me leaning toward Russell. I didn't know if I was physically leaning, but it felt as if I were on a cellular level. There was a tug in my heart as he looked down at me.

I was used to feeling small because I *was* short. However, I wasn't accustomed to the feeling Russell elicited—this desire to let myself tumble into his strength. I was so used to wanting to catch up, to be fast, to be strong, to be quick, to prove myself like the little sister I was. And then later, the tomboy turning into a woman who'd fallen in love with a career primarily dominated by men. I wanted to forget that urge just now.

And somehow, Russell gave me that permission. That should've given me pause and made me more sensible. Yet I'd already been colossally unsensible with him.

I didn't know who moved first, but we both moved toward each other, erasing the distance between us. I could hear the rush of blood in my ears as the echoing beat of my heart reverberated through my entire body. Heat spun in fiery pinwheels as little bonfires alighted throughout me.

His dark eyes searched mine, and the only relief I felt at this moment was seeing the need in his gaze mirroring mine. I couldn't hide it. Sweet hell, I wanted this man so badly. My need was a fist pounding on the door.

"Tell me something," he murmured, his words barely breaking through. "Is it crazy for us to do this again?"

Well, now, that was a really sensible question, but I wasn't having it, not right now. I lifted my chin. "We already did the crazy thing. We can't undo it," I returned, pointing out the obvious.

His low chuckle cinched the need tighter inside me. He lifted a hand, brushing a wayward lock of hair off my cheek. Hot shivers chased down my side as his fingers brushed the sensitive shell of my ear when he tucked the hair behind it.

His palm was warm as it slid along my neck, his thumb tracing a blazing path over my collarbone. Who knew that was an erogenous zone? It was certainly news to me. But oh, my god, his touch there was a ticklish pleasure that sent licks of fire racing over my skin. Time sped up and slowed down when he dipped his head, his lips following the path of his thumb. He dropped fiery kisses on my collarbone. His teeth grazed along the sensitive skin where my shoulder met my neck, and I shivered against him, letting out a shameless moan.

He murmured something I couldn't even register, and then his mouth was on mine. We tumbled into a kiss—licks, nips, ragged breaths, and then diving back into each other. I couldn't get enough of him as I plastered myself to him, an arm snaking around his waist with my fingers pressing into the corded muscles along his spine. His palm slid in a path down my back, cupping my bottom and pulling me fast against his arousal. I moaned into his mouth, and he broke free, gulping in air as he murmured something indecipherable.

I breathed in deep lungfuls of the crisp autumn air. Another owl called, and this time, a raven answered in the rapidly falling darkness. Suddenly, I heard the sounds of tires on gravel, and headlights illuminated us in an arc as a vehicle turned into the parking area. I didn't even have enough sense to jump away. I didn't really care.

Russell appeared to have a modicum of control and stepped back, slightly turning and catching my hand in his. "Let's go."

We walked the short distance to his truck. Some teenagers spilled out of the car that parked nearby, ignoring us completely as they proceeded to build a campfire on the beach.

Russell and I climbed into the truck. He made sure I was buckled up before backing out. The drive back to the house was in complete silence. As far as words were concerned, that was. He reached across the console, his palm landing on my thigh, his touch a hot brand. Meanwhile, my body was a cacophony of sensation as need rampaged through me restlessly. By the time we got back to the house, I was tied in knots of lust. I could feel the slick arousal between my thighs, and my nipples were chafing against my bra. We tumbled out together, and he caught my hand as we ran across the gravel and into the house. The door slammed shut behind us, my back pressing against it instantly when he caged me in his arms and pinned me to the door, kissing me as if I was the very air he needed to breathe.

He took deep sips from my mouth, and I *loved* that he couldn't get enough. Because I definitely couldn't get enough of him. Our tongues dueled, and our kiss was messy and wild. His hands were rough as one pushed my jacket out of the way and slid up under my shirt, his touch was warm against my cool skin. He had my bra undone in a hot second and let out a groan into my mouth when he cupped a breast, pinching the nipple slightly.

My hips rocked into his arousal. We broke apart out of our sheer need for air. His eyes were hot on mine. We stared at each other, our chests rising and falling in rapid breaths. Then it was a race. He stepped away from the door, shoving my coat off my arms as I pushed at his. My shirt came off first, then my bra fell somewhere between the entryway and the kitchen.

We didn't make it upstairs or downstairs. A few seconds or minutes later, his hand was reaching between my thighs, and he let out a growl. "Fuck, you're so wet." His fingers delved into me.

The insides of my thighs were damp from my arousal. We never even got our boots off. My jeans were shoved down just past my hips when he bent me over the counter. The tight friction created from where they banded around my thighs had my pussy clenching at the sensation. I was slippery wet and needy, so fucking needy.

I felt the velvety heat of his arousal brushing against my thigh and arched back. The granite counter was cool under my belly and breasts as his fingers teased into my folds. His lips were hot as he dropped a line of kisses down my spine. I trembled under his touch, shamelessly begging, "Please."

Abruptly, he stopped, and I looked over my shoulder, almost angry. "What?" I barked out.

"I need to get a condom," he replied, his voice sounding strangled.

I swallowed. "I'm on the pill."

His eyes widened slightly. "Are you sure?"

"Of course, I'm sure. I take it every day. I promise I'm clean too. I don't get tons of action if you were wondering." He gave me a long stare. "Do I need to be concerned about you?"

He shook his head swiftly. "No. I swear, I always use condoms."

"Well, if you insist. I'll wait." I rested my elbows on the counter and took a deep breath.

He stayed quiet for a beat, and then said, "If you trust me, I trust you."

I felt the thick crown of him pressing at my entrance, and I let out another shameless moan as I arched into him. With the friction of my thighs being pressed together by my jeans, the thick slide of him filling me was intense. One of his hands gripped my hip, and I felt his forehead press between my shoulder blades.

His speech was slurred when he said, "Oh, fuck. That feels good. Oh, my God."

He seated himself more deeply, and I pushed back into him. He held still for a long moment. I was already teetering on the edge of my climax and felt my channel rippling around him.

## Chapter Nineteen
# RUSSELL

I tried to hold my release at bay, but it was nearly impossible. Being bare inside Paisley was intoxicating. Her silky slick channel clenched around me as I took several deep breaths. I finally lifted my head from where it was resting between her shoulder blades.

Opening my eyes, I stared down at her. Her back had freckles scattered over it, and her bottom was round and lush. She arched and pressed back into me, her auburn hair a tangle around her shoulders. Gritting my teeth, I took a breath and drew back, letting out a ragged groan as I filled her again.

Abruptly, she went still, her hands clenching on the counter. She cried out, a sharp, keening sound as her pussy convulsed around me. I tumbled over the edge after her. My balls drew up tightly as my release sizzled through me like hot lightning. I poured into her, jerking roughly. My mind was hazed. I was almost dizzy from it as I curled over her, resting a palm on the counter and trying to catch my breath.

After a few moments, I opened my eyes and

uncurled my hand from her hip, smoothing my palm up her side. An intense sense of intimacy stole through me. I dipped my head because I couldn't resist kissing along the sweet curve of her neck. She turned her head, arching into my touch like a cat.

When I lifted my head, my gaze collided with Paisley's. We stared at each other quietly for a moment. I thought maybe this should feel awkward, but it didn't. I straightened, my hand sliding down her back again. Right then, her stomach growled, and she bit her lip. Her cheeks went pink, and my heart turned over in my chest.

"I think I'm hungry," she murmured huskily.

I felt my lips kick up into a smile. "You think?" I teased.

I slowly drew back, almost regretfully. Being buried deep inside Paisley was a kind of heaven I'd never imagined. We got dressed, and even she laughed about the scattered random mess of our clothes. It said something about how out of control my need had been that neither one of us had gotten fully undressed.

It was a damn crime that she had to pull her jeans up. Her bottom was perfect, and she even had freckles there. I had plans for that bottom. I needed to kiss every freckle, for starters.

"What are you having for dinner?" I asked.

She looked at me, biting her lip. "Well, if you weren't here, I would probably make something from a box."

I grinned. "How about I make something?"

We stared at each other for a long moment. We seemed to be doing a lot of that. She nodded.

"Let's shower first," I added.

She bit her lip but followed along. After we'd showered and changed, we returned to the kitchen. "Okay, what are you going to make?" she asked.

"I don't know. Let me see what we've got." She looked at me like that was crazy. "What?" I prompted as I crossed to the refrigerator and opened it, perusing the contents.

"You're just going to think of something?"

Glancing over my shoulder as I closed the refrigerator and opened the pantry cabinet, I nodded. "Yes. That's a thing that people sometimes do."

She let out a little huff. "Whatever. I don't cook a lot. You know that."

"Really?" I teased.

"I'll be your assistant," she offered. "Just tell me what to do. You already know I can grate cheese like a pro."

"I do know that. How about I make something with this chicken?" I pulled out a package of chicken. "I'll make some seasoned rice with it."

"Does it involve grating cheese?" Paisley asked. Her expression was so earnest I wanted to hug her.

She liked to feel competent, and it was so obvious she just didn't when it came to anything in the kitchen. She was highly proficient at work. I'd been working with her now going on six weeks, and she was an excellent firefighter. I felt a twinge of guilt. Because the second I'd laid eyes on her at her interview and thought she was hot, I'd gotten uncomfortable about it. I'd tried to act like she wasn't a good hire. She was rock-solid, she had great judgment, and she was absolutely a team player. Except when she was arguing with me, but maybe we had a way to avoid arguing.

She cleared her throat, and I realized my mind had wandered, but then it tended to do that with Paisley.

"Right. This doesn't involve a lot of cheese, but

that's okay. You can do other things. Should we have some beer?"

"I thought I told you I don't like beer?"

"You did tell me that. I keep forgetting because you seem like the kind of person who would like beer."

Her brows hitched up in question, and I shrugged. "I'm going to have a beer. Would you like something to drink?"

"I got some wine the other day. You should've told me you wanted some beer, and I would've picked some up for you."

"We weren't really talking for a few days there," I replied.

Her cheeks went pink. "We weren't purposely not talking," she said.

"No, but we were avoiding each other enough that we couldn't talk," I added as I pulled the chicken out of the fridge.

I fetched a beer and handed her a wine glass. I set to prepping the meal and gave her the task of pounding the chicken breasts with a meat tenderizer. "Why am I doing this?" she asked as she settled into her task.

"Because I'm going to roll them with filling."

"Oh, with what?"

"It'll involve a little cheese, so you can grate some next. I promise it'll be delicious."

When Paisley smiled over at me, my heart did that funny tumble that seemed solely associated with her. I didn't know what it meant, but I knew it felt unsettling. Also unsettling was the fact we'd had a really great day. Of course, having mind-blowing sex in the kitchen made the day even better.

It was only when the house phone rang after we'd finished eating and were lounging at the kitchen table playing Scrabble that I realized I'd completely forgotten about her brother's phone call, the very thing that had set us off on our trip to the beach. Based on the look on her face, I was pretty sure she hadn't thought about it either.

## Chapter Twenty
## PAISLEY

My brother's phone call had totally slipped my mind. As I watched Russell cross the kitchen to answer the phone mounted on the wall, I realized I had him to thank for that. He was the one who'd said we should go for a hike. I'd had a really great day, and I actually liked hanging out with Russell. Plus, crazy hot sex was a bonus I hadn't even considered.

My heart felt funny, and my belly swooped as if I were falling from a great height. Oh wow, I wasn't supposed to be feeling things for Russell. Yet here I was with lots of *feelings* bouncing around inside.

"Hello," he said after he lifted the phone.

Reality punched me hard again, right in the chest.

"Hey, Mom," Russell said easily. "You don't usually call this number."

As soon as he spoke, the tension that had drawn tight inside me loosened. I took a breath before lifting my wineglass and draining the last of it. My eyes traveled around the table. Our empty plates had been pushed to the center, and there was a balled-up napkin beside mine. My feet were propped on a chair, and I wiggled my toes. Somewhere along the way, I'd finally removed my boots. I flushed as I recalled our rush earlier. Wow. My belly trembled, and heat raced through me at the recollection of our near frantic encounter.

"Just tell them to come by on Monday. Both of us will be at work. We're on duty so they don't need to worry about our schedule."

A moment later, he was hanging up the phone and walking back across the kitchen. My eyes soaked him in. Good grief. Russell was too sexy for his own good. His muscled shoulders filled out his T-shirt. I tracked his easy stride and the way his jeans clung lovingly to his thighs.

I wanted him all over again. I was feeling greedy. I also wanted to be distracted again. Now that I'd tossed all reason out the window when it came to Russell, I didn't care to hold my need at bay. When he stopped beside my chair and looked down, I hooked a finger around his belt loop, giving him a little tug when I glanced up. Without a word, I watched his eyes darken.

Sliding my hand down, I caressed over his fly, gratified at the harsh sound of his breath hissing through his teeth and the feel of his arousal swelling under my palm. "I think we need to take our time this time," I murmured as I flicked the buttons open.

He watched me quietly, his nostrils flaring when I dragged his boxers down, and his cock sprang free. I trailed one finger along the underside of his shaft. A bead of cum rolled from the tip, and I swiped it with my finger, sucking it clean as I looked up at him.

"Paisley," he growled, his tone almost strangled.

"Yes?" I teased as I leaned forward and swirled my

tongue around the crown of his cock before sucking it in.

His hand laced in my hair, gripping tightly. He took me at my word and let me take my time. Then he carried me upstairs, and he took *his* time, spreading me out on the bed and treating me like his personal feast. When I felt his shoulders press my thighs apart, he whispered, "Your turn."

I forgot everything else, even my name, except for when he nearly shouted it after he buried himself inside me again, filling me in deep pumps. I came for the third time that evening. We slept together again, and when I woke up the following morning, I thought maybe I needed to find a way to get sensible right quick.

But then, his palm splayed over my belly as he rose on an elbow and his navy eyes met mine.

"Maybe we should set some ground rules," I murmured.

My belly trembled under his touch, and my core clenched because I already wanted him again. His brows hitched, but he nodded.

I forged ahead. "Okay. We can't tell anybody about us. That's the first one."

"Okay."

"No strings, right?" My heart gave a wobbly thump with that question.

I was trying to make sure this stayed casual even though I sensed I was already past that. Maybe if I set some rules and made them explicit, I could follow them.

Russell's eyes searched mine before he nodded slowly. "I'm on board with no strings, but if we're seeing other people, I think we should use condoms," he said.

That was rather practical of him. I blinked. "Well, I'm not seeing anybody else, and I don't intend to."

"Okay, so we're *exclusively* no strings?" he prompted, his lips kicking up at a corner.

"Yes." My lips tugged into a smile, and a giggle escaped.

The next thing I knew, he caught my hands in his and stretched them above my head. I forgot everything else except us.

---

A few days later, I saw a shirtless Russell walking through the workout area at the station. I glanced over, and our eyes met. Every cell in my body clamored for him, but we'd set the rules. I couldn't do anything. Not now. Certainly not at work.

I *knew* I stared at him too long, and I recognized the second he became aware of that small problem. His lips kicked up at one corner, and I forced myself to look away and keep walking. Being a hotshot firefighter, a profession dominated mostly by men, meant we hung out at the station together a lot. We all worked out because we had to stay in shape. Being in peak physical form was a requirement for this job, and our lives depended on it. Every fire station in the country had workout areas. I had never—*never*—even paid attention to the guys working out. I noticed them with about as much interest as seeing Maisie answer the phone out front. Yet I was practically drooling over Russell.

Feeling flustered, I hurried down the hall and turned into the women's locker area. Blessedly, it was empty. I closed the door, rested my back against it, and let my hips slide down. The cool metal of the door sifted through my shirt, a contrast to the heat coming off me in waves. Someone tried to open the door, and I stood quickly, practically bolting across the room. A second later, the door opened, and Susannah commented, "Well, that was weird."

I glanced over. "What?" I hoped my voice sounded nonchalant, but I could feel the blaze of heat in my cheeks.

Susannah looked at me and back at the door. She was about to close it when a voice called, "Susannah!"

She peered back into the hallway. "Hey-yyy!"

A second later, a woman I hadn't met appeared. She had glossy dark hair and big blue eyes. She tugged Susannah into a quick hug before stepping back and glancing in my direction. She smiled over at me. "Hey, I'm Harlow. You must be new."

I crossed over, holding my hand out because I didn't know what else to do. Harlow shook her head. "Oh no, you get a hug. Women firefighters have to hang together."

She gave me a quick squeeze, and I was laughing when she stepped back. "It's not fight club, but hug club," I teased.

Susannah closed the door. "Sounds about right to me." She sat down on a bench across from me, announcing, "We need to have girl talk."

Harlow immediately sat down beside me. "What's up? I'm totally out of the loop."

"Well, first off, this is Paisley. She's on the new crew that Graham's heading up."

"More firefighters? Just what this town needs," Harlow teased.

Susannah smiled over at me. "I am so glad you got hired. It was down to Phoebe and me around here after Harlow left."

"You used to be a firefighter?"

Harlow nodded. "Sure did. I loved it."

"Then she fell in love," Susannah teased.

Harlow's cheeks went a little pink. "I did. I got married, and now we're *maybe* thinking about a baby." Her gaze bounced to Susannah. "I don't even know how you manage this job with a toddler."

Susannah shrugged as though it was no big deal. "I try to act as if I have it together, but most of the time, I don't. I've discovered being a parent is constantly lowering the bar for myself. I know if I didn't have Ward to help, it would feel beyond overwhelming sometimes, and I couldn't do this job."

"Ward's awesome. He's totally got it bad for you," Harlow gushed with a grin.

Susannah flushed. "He still doesn't love it that I'm on the town crew. We'd never see each other if we were on different hotshot crews, or we'd be gone at the same time if we were on the same one. This way, I'm always here. When he's not out in the backcountry, we see each other all the time. How is Max?"

Harlow smiled. "He's good. He's with me and chatting out front. He pretends it intimidates him to come here."

"He's not a firefighter?" I interjected.

"He's a tech billionaire." Harlow rolled her eyes. "I still can't believe we got married. Enough about me. What's the girl talk about?"

Susannah immediately looked toward me, her eyebrows hitching up. "I don't actually know, but you were almost drooling over Russell out there. What the hell is going on?"

I was pretty sure my blush had receded by then, but my cheeks were fiery hot in an instant. I stared at her, swallowing. "What do you mean?"

"Oh, don't try to play dumb with me." Susannah actually wagged her finger, her strawberry blond curls bouncing when she laughed.

Harlow looked from her to me. "I feel like she's put you on the spot, and you just met me."

I rolled my eyes and let out a sigh. "I've only been here for a month. It was much better when Russell and I were fighting."

"You were fighting?"

"Russell's a pretty easy guy to deal with," Susannah offered.

"Have I met Russell?" Harlow asked.

Susannah shrugged. "I don't know. He got hired on to the new crew too, but he's from Willow Brook. He's a standard-issue Alaska guy—tall, strong, and firefighter hot. He's not my type, but he's totally Paisley's type."

Putting my face in my hands, I let out a groan. Harlow reached over and rubbed her hand up and down my back. I decided then she was a good person. "It'll be okay. Susannah fell for her boss, and they were on a crew together. She cannot give you shit about this, trust me."

I lifted my head. "Really? Obviously, I know you're both firefighters, but I didn't know he was your crew superintendent before."

Susannah simply shrugged. "It used to embarrass me, but I'm way over it now."

I looked between them, deciding to abandon all attempts at playing it cool. "What do you know about Russell?"

Susannah laughed. "Well, almost everything. We grew up in Willow Brook together. He's a nice guy. Do you just have the hots for him, or do you have feelings for him?"

"I'm not sure," I answered, which was the truth even though I didn't want to admit it.

"That makes things complicated," Harlow offered.

I sighed and leaned back against the lockers. Lifting one hand idly, I caught an open locker door and traced my fingers along the metal edge. The door to the locker room opened again. This time, Phoebe appeared and looked amongst us as she let the door fall closed behind her.

"Well, hey. What's up?"

Susannah patted the bench beside her. "Have a seat. Girl talk. Everything said in this room is in the cone."

"The cone?" I prompted.

Phoebe laughed. "This must be about you and Russell. He couldn't stop staring at you."

Susannah grinned. "I just saw her drooling over his chest."

I groaned and closed my eyes. "This better stay in the cone, whatever the hell that is."

When I opened them again, Susannah placed her palm over her chest. "It's the cone of silence. We won't say a word. If you want, we can even call Maisie back for a huddle."

"Please don't." I shook my head. "I can't deal with it. It's too much."

Susannah looked toward Phoebe. "Paisley was just asking me what I knew about Russell."

Phoebe caught my eyes. "We both went to school with him since kindergarten. Russell's a great guy. His mom is friends with mine. The thing with his dad was a heartbreaker last year."

"What happened?" I asked, honestly curious.

"He was on the town crew for years. His gear

broke, and he fell off a cliff when he was out climbing. Russell arrived on the scene after it happened."

"Oh, God," I breathed, pressing my hand on my chest over my heart.

"It was awful. His mom was devastated," Susannah added.

"He's been pretty quiet about it. As far as I know, he's never really had a serious relationship. He's not a jerk, but he is a flirt. Has anything happened? And what do you want?" Phoebe asked.

"Definitely no complications," I said firmly, avoiding her other question.

"Well, you might not want to look at him when you're at work then," Susannah suggested, her voice lilting up at the end.

I burst out laughing, and I knew my face was bright red. "Okay, no looking at him. I can handle that."

At that moment, there was a knock on the door, and a man's voice filtered through. "Hey, it's Graham. I'm supposed to let Harlow know that Maisie wants her to come out front now that she's off the phone."

Harlow chuckled as she stood. "Can we get together while I'm in town?"

"Of course! How long will you be here?" Susannah asked.

"A week."

"Let's make it happen. We can meet at Wildlands or do cards one night."

Before another word was said, the door burst open, and Maisie was standing there. She snatched Harlow into a hug. "You just waved and walked by me," she protested when she stepped back.

"You were on the phone," Harlow explained.

Maisie grinned. "I know. Moving on, random

gossip nugget." She glanced between Susannah and Phoebe. "Who's Mae Townsend?"

Rowan Cole happened to be walking by in the hallway and came to a quick stop. Maisie gave him a puzzled look. "What?"

"Nothing." Rowan shook his head quickly and kept walking.

Maisie pursed her lips and arched a brow. "That was *not* nothing. Anyway, who the hell is Mae Townsend?"

Susannah answered, "She grew up in Willow Brook, went to college in North Carolina, and only comes back to town for visits. Why do you ask?"

"Apparently, her grandmother is really sick."

"Oh, no. I'm so sorry about that." Susannah looked amongst us. "Her grandmother is Carrie Dodge's sister. Pretty private and even bossier than Carrie."

Maisie's brow furrowed. "Oh, wow. I'll have to check on Carrie." The dispatch line rang through Maisie's headphones, which she held in her hand. "I gotta get back out front." She looked over at me. "And Russell keeps staring at your ass." At that, she hustled out while putting her headset on and answering the call.

Phoebe, Susannah, and Harlow burst into laughter. Meanwhile, my cheeks were hot all over again.

## Chapter Twenty-One
# RUSSELL

"You need to stop staring at my ass," Paisley announced.

"Excuse me?"

I turned from where I was sautéeing chicken on the stove. I adjusted the flame to a lower heat and covered the pan. She was sitting on a stool by the counter with her legs crossed and a glass of wine in hand. Her auburn hair was damp from a shower she'd taken after we got home, which I'd shared with her. It had been a most excellent shower. She was wearing one of my T-shirts. I didn't mind admitting I fucking loved seeing her wear my shirt with her leggings and a pair of fuzzy socks with penguins on them. She was adorably sexy.

"I said that you need to stop staring at my ass."

"How would you know I'm staring at your ass?" I countered.

That view was the back of her, so I thought I had a point. Of course, I knew I stared at her ass because it was too tempting not to.

"Because Maisie *and* Phoebe both commented on

it. I'm not putting all the blame on you. Susannah noticed me staring at your chest, so we kind of need to work on that."

"It's hard not to look at you," I said, deciding to go for complete honesty.

Her cheeks went pink, and her lashes swept down. When her gaze lifted to mine again, I wanted to kiss her. I couldn't get enough of her. Having her here, right here, in my house was almost too much. The more time I had with her, the more I wanted her. This was a new experience for me. I'd never lived with a woman I was having crazy hot sex with on the regular.

"Staring at your ass is better than being an ass to you," I quipped.

Paisley rolled her eyes. I chuckled and turned to check on the chicken. After another stir, I added in some seasonings and rice.

"Russell, I don't want *us* to be an issue at work."

"We're not going to be an issue at work. I will stop staring at any part of you, I swear. At least not when anyone's around," I said as I turned back to her.

She rolled her eyes again. "You need to keep your shirt on."

"Sometimes, I take my shirt off when I'm working out," I protested. "All the other guys do. Do you stare at their chests?"

"No. This has never been an issue for me at work, like ever. And there are men everywhere," she said rather vehemently.

The house phone rang, the sound jangling loudly in the room. Our heads swiveled to look at it together. "Don't answer it. Please," Paisley said.

I shrugged. "Okay." I rounded the kitchen island

and rested my hands on either side of her, curling them around the edge of the counter. "What's up with your brother anyway? You don't talk about him."

It was as if clouds passed over Paisley's eyes. She chewed on her bottom lip and shrugged. "I appreciate you asking, but I can't talk about it."

I didn't like her answer, which didn't make sense. We said no strings. Yet here I was, feeling hurt. Because this woman—who I wasn't supposed to want and who I didn't want things to get complicated with —was telling me she didn't want to confide in me about something that obviously hurt her.

I felt like she didn't trust me, and *that* hurt. But I didn't push. Not now. I stepped back, striving to keep my tone nonchalant, as I said, "Understood. If you ever want to talk, just let me know. It doesn't mean anything more than that. I try to be there for my friends."

As soon as I said that, I knew two things. One, I was lying because I felt a lot more for Paisley than friendship. And two, describing her as nothing more than a friend hurt *her*.

A different kind of shadow flickered over her eyes now. I reminded myself she was the one who said she wanted ground rules. She took a gulp of her wine and nodded. "I know. You're a good friend."

I busied myself by checking on the chicken, which was pointless because it needed more time since I'd added the rice. I finally placed the lid over the pan again, asking, "What do you mean I'm a good friend?"

"I've noticed around the station and in the field. All the guys trust you. That's all."

My throat felt tight, and I didn't know why. Suddenly, I thought of my father and how he always got my mother small gifts at random times—flowers or something. Why the hell was I thinking of my father in relation to this conversation with Paisley? Instantly I heard my mother's voice. "*I want you to have something like what I had with your father.*"

My mom had said something along those lines to me probably once a month in the last year. Paisley and I weren't like my parents. We were way too fresh for that, but she was the first woman I'd ever wanted more with. What a clusterfuck this was. We weren't *together*. We were roommates, and she would argue the technicality of that. I needed to remember that.

The phone had gone silent, and it didn't ring again. We shifted gears and ate dinner while I had a beer. We played a game of Scrabble. That was something I'd done with my parents growing up, and Paisley loved it. She wasn't a huge fan of TV. Personally, I would watch just about any sport if it was on, but I wasn't a diehard fan of anything.

We behaved like a couple, except I kept having to remind myself we weren't. We were often tangled up between the sheets in one of our beds, and we usually slept together, which was maybe not too smart. I was growing to like it. A lot.

After that tense conversation, we chilled out. Paisley was the perfect distraction from my thoughts. I didn't have to think about my feelings when I was buried in her silky, clenching core, and when she was shuddering against me. That was the only time she let down her defenses. She was a guarded person in general. I sensed she didn't know what to make of the women around the station trying to befriend her, but she was going along with it. She was friendly, albeit a little reserved.

But when she was naked, and I was chasing her scattered freckles with my hands and my lips and my tongue, she let go. I *loved* seeing that side of her. I was starting to feel restless with the secrecy of it all.

The next day, she left to do a grocery run in Anchorage and even offered to get some things for me. I gave her cash and a list because she was a terrible shopper without a list. I fixed a few things around the house while she was gone and followed up with the guy replacing the water heater in the basement before winter. We were swapping it out with one of those highly efficient propane hot water heaters. We already had separate propane heaters for the different floors. That way, we only had to heat the space we needed rather than the entire house.

After the water heater guy left, I paid some bills and found myself sitting at the kitchen table, drumming my fingertips restlessly. I kept looking at the clock and realized I was waiting for Paisley to get back even though she'd told me she'd be gone all day because she was going with Phoebe and Susannah. I made another pot of coffee, deciding I would head into the station and work out. The phone rang just after I hit the start button on the coffeemaker. I knew how sensitive Paisley was to that house phone. I glanced over at it suspiciously before deciding to answer it. "What the hell?" I murmured to myself. If it was her brother again, maybe I could get some answers from him.

"Hello?"

"Hi, is Paisley around?"

It was definitely her brother. Maybe I'd only answered two other calls from him, but I recognized his voice now.

"She's not around. Can I take a message?"

"Yeah. Could you let her know her brother called?"

"Sure. Mind if I ask a question?"

"No, not at all," he said easily.

"What's your name?"

"Ryder?" He chuckled. "And you are?"

"Russell Dane. How come you don't call Paisley's cell phone?" I thought that was the most obvious question in the fucking universe at this point.

"I prefer landlines. The connection's better," he replied.

"Bullshit. Something's up. Every time you call, Paisley gets all stressed out," I said flatly, my protectiveness flaring.

"Does she now?" Her brother's tone changed subtly, although I sensed he was trying to keep it cool.

"Yeah. Is there anything I should be worried about?"

"Nah. Do me a favor and keep an eye on her, though. I'm just a guy, making sure his little sister's okay."

"Do you even know how I know Paisley?"

"Yeah, you work with her, and she rents a room in your house."

"Look, if you're up to something that might affect Paisley, why don't you keep her out of it?"

I had no fucking clue what was going on, and I was honestly shooting in the dark here, but my spidey sense was tingling.

"Nothing to worry about. I just like to check on my sister and touch base every now and then. If you could give her that message, that'd be great."

"Sure thing."

I hung up the phone then, staring at it for a long moment after I did. As I turned away, my fingers itched to pick up my own cell phone and call Paisley to demand some answers on this. I know she wouldn't appreciate it, and that was putting it mildly. We were getting along a lot better, ever since we turned the tension between us into a blazing fire. But I knew Paisley had a stubborn streak. It was kind of a given as a hotshot firefighter. You had to have a high tolerance for danger and the willingness to stand your ground at times when other people might be more sensible and leave. Paisley had that in spades.

As soon as my coffee was ready, I turned it off and decided to leave it for now. I was going to do a little reconnaissance on my own at Firehouse Café instead. I could stop in and get some coffee, then go work out. Plus, Janet's coffee was always better than mine.

## Chapter Twenty-Two
# RUSSELL

"I don't know," Janet said. She looked over at me, cocking her head to the side. "Why are you asking?"

"Paisley's my roommate, and I work with her," I said, shifting my shoulders slightly.

Janet narrowed her eyes. "You're being nosy. That's not really a guy thing."

"Sorry to break it to you, but you're nosy."

Janet shrugged unabashedly. "I am, but that's *my* thing. I run a coffee shop, and I have to stay up to speed on any rumors. I consider myself the unofficial mother of everyone who comes in here."

I recognized Graham's laughter as he approached from behind me. "That you do. Does Russell need some mothering?"

I rolled my eyes. "No, my own mother does plenty. Not that I mind you mothering me," I rushed to add.

Janet grinned. "I know you don't. You're a good boy. Let me start that coffee."

"What's up?" Graham asked as he rested his hip against the counter.

"I'm getting coffee. What about you?"

"Same," he replied with a shrug. At that moment, the door to the café opened, and his girlfriend entered with his daughter.

"Group outing?"

Graham smiled. "Always." Madison and Allie had stopped as Allie pointed at something on the screen of her phone.

"You seem pretty happy these days," I commented.

Graham looked at me, curling his lips in a slow smile. "I am."

I grinned and cuffed him on the shoulder. "You deserve it, man. Madison's awesome and good for you. You've even been nicer since she's been around."

Graham dipped his chin, shrugging a little sheepishly. "I suppose I am."

"She and Allie seem to be getting along well," I observed as I glanced over at them.

"They are," he agreed.

"Are you officially moving in together yet?" I teased lightly just as Janet passed my coffee to me across the counter. I fished out some cash, handing some to her and stuffing several bills in the tip jar. "If there's any change, you can put the rest in there," I added.

Janet nodded, and Graham glanced at her. "My usual."

Janet winked. "I'll start it and wait for the girls to order."

"I'm covering everything," Graham noted.

Graham looked back at me. "We're not officially moving in together, but I suppose we might as well."

"You were gonna do some work on your place anyway, weren't you?"

"I was planning on it. We're right next door to Madison, so we'll figure out what works best."

At that moment, Madison and Allie made their

way to us. "Hey, Russell," Allie said, bouncing lightly on her feet.

Madison smiled. "Good morning. Did you already order for us?"

Graham shook his head. "I didn't know what you wanted."

Janet chuckled as she handed Graham his coffee. "What will it be, ladies? I know it'll be some kind of hot chocolate for Allie."

While they ordered, I happened to look over when Graham slid his arm around Madison's waist. Even though they were a new couple, the intimacy between them was clear. It *was* good to see Graham with her. He was an absolutely solid guy who'd been raising his daughter by himself since a mere month after she was born.

A hollow feeling passed through my chest. I hadn't been walking around craving a relationship, but just now watching them together, I wondered what it might be like to have that. Of course, the only woman I could think of was Paisley.

My cell phone buzzed, and I glanced down to see a text from my mother, asking me if I could stop by. She needed help moving some furniture in the house, so that would give me something to do. I said my goodbyes and left.

I hadn't counted on my mother bringing up relationships or her opinion of my lack thereof in that regard. My mom was turning one room into her sewing room and needed more light. I was only halfway through moving the guest bedroom furniture from one bedroom to another when she asked if I'd gone on any dates lately.

I looked over at her. "Seriously, Mom?" I grunted as I shouldered through the door with a small dresser in my arms. I set it down by the wall where she'd already directed me.

"What's wrong with me asking about your dating life?"

"Nothing's wrong with it. It's just annoying. In fact, it makes me less likely to share anything about it if you want me to be honest."

My mother sighed. She wrinkled her nose, pressed her lips in a line, and rolled her eyes for good measure. "Fine. Don't let yourself get too old."

"Jesus, Mom. I'm only thirty-one. That's not exactly old."

"When I was your age, you were already seven."

"Well, people got married a lot younger and had kids a lot younger back then," I countered.

"Graham has Allie," she offered pointedly.

"Oh, my God, Mom. Graham has Allie because he got his girlfriend pregnant in high school. Don't get me wrong, he's an incredible dad, but I doubt that's what you were hoping I was planning on. Also, it's too late for that because I'm well past high school. Dad lectured me about birth control more than once and used Graham as an example for crying out loud."

My mother laughed. "Very true. How is it working out with Paisley at the lake house?"

She had *that* tone, one I knew well. She was trying to be all casual, but my mom was terrible about that. She was totally being nosy.

"Paisley's fine. Anything else you want to know about Paisley while you're asking?"

My mom shrugged slightly, looking out the windows like she didn't even care about our conversation, which I knew was bullshit. "Do you mind having her at the lake house?"

I walked past my mom and down the hallway to

fetch her new sewing table from the garage. When I returned a moment later, I replied, "Of course I don't mind her at the house."

I wasn't about to fill my mom in on the details of just how little I minded having Paisley around. Of course, thinking about Paisley brought back that call with her brother and her reluctance to even talk about him.

"Well, I'm glad it's working out for her to be there. You know how hard it is to find a rental around here in the winter."

"It's hard all the time, Mom," I pointed out.

She nodded. "I know. Thank you for dealing with the water heater guy."

"Of course. Switching to the on-demand water heater is a good move. It will definitely save us some money on heating expenses."

My mom's phone rang, distracting her and leaving me to put everything away on my own. I was just finishing up when my phone buzzed again. I glanced down at the screen, surprised to see a text from Paisley.

Paisley: *What kind of beer did you want me to get at the store?*

I chuckled. She was not a fan of beer. I quickly typed out a response. As I slid my phone back in my pocket, I realized it made me way too happy to have her pick up beer for me. There was an intimacy to mundane errands.

Fuck. Things were feeling complicated.

## Chapter Twenty-Three
# PAISLEY

"Um, I talked to him just last week. Surely, you've seen him around town since then?" I prompted.

I'd just started driving after Phoebe and Susannah dropped me off at my car at an exit near the highway where we'd met up before driving together for our shopping trip. I could practically picture my mother's face right then. There would be a little crease between her brows, and she would blink before she could press her lips together.

"I haven't seen your brother around town. And, you know, I'm worried," my mother replied.

"Worried about what?" I countered, trying to keep my tone light while my gut was churning.

"A mother's intuition. I don't have any reason, but I just have a bad feeling about what's going on."

"What's going on? I don't even know what you're talking about, Mom."

I didn't specifically, but then I did.

"Nothing's adding up. Your brother's constantly traveling for work. He doesn't stay in touch like he used to, and I ran into Chris. You know, his old friend?

He looks terrible and was vague when we spoke. Ryder doesn't even play in the local baseball league anymore like he used to. When I asked him about it, he lied to me. I know there's tension between the two of you as well. Can you tell me what's going on?"

I clenched my teeth to keep from groaning out loud. It was true that I'd wanted to move to Alaska anyway. It was true that I loved being a hotshot firefighter. Yet it was also true that I had been beyond relieved to discover an opportunity to leave my hometown and put over two thousand miles between me and the mess my brother had created. I didn't like lying for him, and I hated knowing the truth.

"Mom, I think you should talk to Ryder. We've had our ups and downs. He doesn't love my career choice and thinks it's too risky."

That was also true, and that was fucking rich coming from him—a guy whose accidental career choice was a designer drug dealer.

My mother clucked—she actually clucked. "Paisley, your job *is* risky. We know you love it, so we support it, but your brother worries."

Oh. My. God. She had no idea the mess he was dealing with, yet she was siding with him on his worries about my career.

"Ri-iiight," I said slowly. "Tell me how Dad's doing." Changing the subject was my best option to stop this interrogation.

"He's busy as ever. That drug case is wearing him down, and it worries me."

"I know, I know," I offered soothingly. "Tell him I miss him. I need to go, Mom. I love you both."

"Love you too, honey. Talk to you next week."

The line went quiet in my car, and I tapped to turn the speakers off before letting out a heavy sigh. My hands were clenched on the steering wheel. I stretched my fingers and shook the tension loose. I was tempted to call my brother, so very tempted, but I refused. He was going to have to figure this out. A few minutes later, I turned onto Main Street in Willow Brook. Maybe I'd only been here a short while, but it was starting to feel good to come home.

The sign for Firehouse Café was bright and cheerful in the late afternoon. I saw Maisie walking down the street with a coffee in one hand and her son's hand in her other. She lifted her coffee cup as I passed by with a wave. As I drove past Willow Brook Fire & Rescue, my lips tugged into a smile.

Now that Russell and I had managed the tension between us—if burning it off skin to skin was "managing" it—I felt good about work. Well, minus the temptation to ogle Russell. I'd have to be more careful.

As I drove past Wildlands and turned down the road that led to the lake house, a subtle sizzle of anticipation vibrated through my body. I wondered if Russell would be home, and I was already impatient for tonight. During the day, we were keeping our boundaries clear, but all bets were off at night. Those hours were ours.

## Chapter Twenty-Four
# RUSSELL

I was in the middle of checking on the chicken I was roasting when I heard the door open. As soon as I heard footsteps entering the kitchen, awareness sizzled up my spine, and the hairs on the back of my neck stood.

Paisley was carrying a giant box, and I hurried to take it from her. "Why'd you carry that in? It's too big for you," I scolded as I slid it on the counter.

Her cheeks were pink from the cool air as she shook her arms out. "I overestimated the length of my arms, but I got it in here."

I looked down at her arms and smiled. "They're not as long as mine."

"No shit," she teased.

"I'll help you unload," I said, following her when she turned to walk out again.

I was stepping into a pair of boots by the door as she answered, "You don't have to."

"Already on the way."

I was wearing a short-sleeve T-shirt over my jeans, and I shivered the second I stepped outside. We were deep into fall, which meant chilly evenings with early sunsets. The temperature tended to drop fast once the sun disappeared from the sky.

"How'd your shopping trip go?" I asked when we stopped at the back of her car.

I immediately reached for another large box. Paisley shrugged when I glanced her way. "It was a shopping trip. I went grocery shopping, and Phoebe and Susannah took me to a little café, and I got a salmon burger. They were out of halibut, though."

"Ah, halibut's good. I should make some. Have you had fresh halibut?"

She shook her head when she reached for the door with her free hand. She was carrying a smaller box and held it open for me while I walked through. "I haven't. Tell me what you do with halibut."

We set the boxes down on the counter and started putting away the groceries. "We have plenty of options. A local favorite is halibut tacos."

Paisley's eyes brightened. "I love tacos."

"That's what we're having for dinner tomorrow night then."

When she looked up at me with her pretty jade eyes and pink freckled cheeks, I wanted to kiss her, so I did. Her lips were cool but warmed instantly as soon as they met mine.

I couldn't resist a quick glide of my tongue against hers before straightening. Her cheeks were even pinker now.

"Well, hello," she murmured.

I grinned. "It's good to see you."

After I finished helping her unload the groceries, she poured a glass of wine and sat down on a stool across from me while I finished getting dinner ready.

When I pulled the roast chicken out of the oven, she exclaimed, "Oh, wow, you made one of those yourself!"

"It's not that hard, I swear."

"It seems like it."

"I'd offer to teach you to roast a chicken, but I'm thinking you wouldn't go for it."

She shrugged. "I don't think cooking is for me."

"It's just a matter of learning."

She eyed me skeptically and took a long swallow of her wine. "I enjoy having you cook for me. You're such a manly man."

"Should I get an apron?" I teased.

"Maybe."

After we finished eating, the blasted phone rang again, and I suddenly recalled her brother's message. "Your brother wanted me to let you know he called."

Our relaxed evening dissipated. It felt as if a cold wind blew through the room.

"Oh. When did he call?"

"Not long after you left."

I wanted her to talk about whatever weirdness was going on with him, but I didn't want to push. "He told me to keep an eye on you," I added. While he had said that, as soon as I relayed it, guilt jabbed me. I was frustrated she wouldn't explain, which confused me because she didn't owe me anything. We'd said "no strings."

Yet I thought we were at least friends, even though I knew I felt a lot more than friendly toward her. My heart felt a little achy, and I ignored it.

Paisley took another swallow of her wine. "He likes to play the big-brother role now and then," she finally said.

"Can I ask you something?" As soon as my question slipped out, I bit back a curse. Asking anything was probably going to annoy her.

She surprised me, though. "Go for it."

"Why doesn't your brother call your cell phone? I mean, it's kind of a miracle we even have a landline here. Do you even know the number?"

Paisley leaned her head back and let out a sigh, shaking her head back and forth as she lifted it and met my eyes again. "No, I don't. I know you want to know what's going on with my brother, but I promised him I wouldn't say anything to anyone. He doesn't call my cell because I blocked him. And if that doesn't tell you enough about how fucked up our relationship is, then I don't know what will."

Worry twisted in my chest. "Are you okay? Should I be concerned?" Uneasiness slithered through me.

She shook her head quickly. "My brother's an idiot and made some poor choices. I got caught in the middle between him and my parents, but that's not why I came here. For anyone who likes to work outdoors, Alaska is a dream. Coming here was definitely on my bucket list, but it was also convenient because I could get away from dealing with him. You don't need to worry about me. I appreciate you passing on the messages for my brother. I don't even know how he got this number."

"I'm sure he looked it up. My parents used to rent this place out every summer, so the info's available online."

Paisley chewed on her bottom lip. Even though I was unsettled with how I felt about her and whatever the hell was going on with her brother, I was relieved. I wished she'd tell me more, and it stung a little that she wouldn't tell me the whole story. But at least she was honest enough to give me an outline of the situation.

Even with all of that spinning through my mind, when she bit her lip, my thoughts derailed. Fuck me. This woman was tapped into the heartbeat of my desire.

"I get it." I heard myself saying, somehow managing to keep the conversation on track.

Paisley's eyes lifted to mine, a mix of uncertainty and guilt swirling there. Her brow furrowed slightly, and she kept worrying her bottom lip before she finally let it go.

I swallowed, feeling a strange tightness banding across my chest.

"You do?" she pressed.

"I think so. Obviously, I don't understand all the details, but I understand someone asking you to keep something private, and I respect that."

The phone stopped ringing, and we both swiveled to look at it for a moment. "I should probably just unblock him on my cell phone," she said.

"Maybe not. This is a way to have a break from him. When you're not here, you don't have to worry about unexpected calls."

She smiled just a little. "That's why I blocked him."

She took a shaky breath, letting it out before reaching over, catching my hand, and lacing her fingers with mine. I didn't know when I'd walked around the counter to her, but there I was.

I stepped closer and lifted my free hand to palm her cheek.

Her eyes searched mine. "How are we doing on the no strings thing?"

"Ah, now that's a good question," I returned. "I

haven't had a chance to demonstrate that I'm not staring at your ass at work yet."

Paisley burst out laughing. The sound of her throaty chuckle sizzled like lightning through my body. Before I knew it, I was capturing the last of her laughter in a kiss and forgetting everything else. As I fell asleep that night in her bed, I recalled her question about our "no strings" agreement. It felt as if she had set tiny darts in my heart, each one tied to a string.

Fuck. I didn't know how to do this. I hadn't planned on falling for Paisley. I thought we'd have fun and stop arguing. We *were* having fun, and we weren't arguing, but it was getting complicated—fast.

## Chapter Twenty-Five
# PAISLEY

Another week passed, and autumn took hold. The days were getting shorter and the nights longer and colder. Although I was never cold at night. Not with Russell. He was my personal furnace, and I was starting to get attached.

This was new for me. I'd never been with a guy who I actually liked this much. It didn't help one bit to have our nights together be so fucking hot it was a miracle we didn't set the house on fire.

After almost a full week of not hearing from my brother, he called three days running. I finally broke down and called him from my cell phone.

"What the hell is going on?" I asked as soon as he answered.

"Thanks for finally answering."

"I'm not answering. I'm calling you. I have a life, you know."

"I know you do."

"What's going on?"

Ryder's sigh filtered through the line. "I'm in some trouble."

My stomach twisted with anxiety. "What else is new? You're dealing designer drugs. And maybe, I don't know for sure, but I'm pretty sure you're deep into that drug ring Dad's office is investigating," I said flatly.

My brother's silence answered for me. I could feel his guilt reverberating through the airwaves of our cell phone connection. "Am I right?" I pressed.

"Yeah," he said, his tone curt.

"You need to get out of that mess."

"I'm working on it. I promise. I'm going out of town, and I need you to cover for me with Mom and Dad."

Nausea rose swiftly in my throat, and I took a deep breath. "If they ask me, I'll just tell them I don't know where you are, but if they ask me more, I won't lie."

Another sigh from my brother. "I know. I'm not going to tell you where I am. I'm going to tell them I'm going on vacation."

"Why are you leaving town?"

"Because there's a problem. A bunch of money and product went missing."

"You know, when you work with criminals, things like this happen."

"Paisley, I don't need a fucking lecture," he snapped.

"Fuck you," I said hotly. "I'm afraid for you. I'm no high and mighty person. For some people, dealing drugs is their only way out of poverty, but that's not what happened to you. I don't even know how you got into this, and every time I think too hard about it, I feel sick."

"It was just some fun in college, easy money."

"And how's it working out now?" My throat was tight, and my chest ached.

Ryder's laugh was bitter. "Not so great, but I'm gonna skip town for a little bit. Take some distance, and I'll figure it out."

"Did *you* steal money?" I surprised myself by asking.

"Fuck no, I wouldn't do that."

I almost laughed, but I felt too sick and upset. "You know, Ryder, I didn't think you'd be doing this, so excuse me for being curious."

"I think I know who did, and that's part of the problem."

"I thought you were pretty high up in this food chain." Since I'd accidentally stumbled across what the fuck my brother was doing, I'd tiptoed around asking him too much, but I was feeling more than done with that. I remembered that afternoon so clearly. He'd been out of town for a weekend and asked me to check on his apartment. While I was there, some guys had shown up at his house and had a "business transaction" in his kitchen. They hadn't even known I was there. I'd hidden in the bathroom, where the cat liked to nap in the sink. She loved the round shape of it. My brother—because he was a sweet guy and more than a drug dealer—didn't even use that bathroom sink because he always wanted it to be dry for her.

"It's not working out, and I'm working on finding a way to unwind this whole thing."

"Ryder, the kind of people you're dealing with aren't the kind you can just walk away from."

"Maybe, maybe not, but I'll figure it out."

"Maybe you should talk to Dad."

"Are you fucking insane?" he retorted.

"I guess I am," I muttered. "Do I need to be worried about anything else other than everything I'm worried about with you? I've been freaked out ever since you called me about that guy."

"No, you should be fine. He got arrested in California, so he's completely out of the loop. He had a record there, so he's in for plenty of time. I'm going to fall off the radar, and I'll be in touch when I can. I'm going to turn this number off, so don't try to reach me at it again."

"How the hell am I supposed to call you if I need to?"

"I'll use burner phones and call you."

My stomach was a whirling dervish of anxiety. Burner phones? What the hell?

"Do I need to be worried about my own numbers getting leaked?"

"No, Paisley. That's the point of burner phones. I use them for a short time and destroy them. I don't keep anyone's information in my contacts." My brother shifted gears abruptly, something he'd done forever. "That Russell guy seems nice."

"Yeah, he is."

"Are you dating him?"

I almost choked. "Uh, no."

My brother chuckled. "I have a vibe that you might not be telling me the truth. Whatever."

"He's my roommate. That's it. And he *is* a good guy. We also work together."

"So it would be complicated if you did date?"

"Definitely. We're friends," I insisted even though it was a lie. We were more than friends, and also, we weren't. It was complicated, but I didn't say any of that to my brother. "I love you, Ryder. Stay safe."

"I will. Love you too."

We ended the call, and I leaned my head back. I was sitting in my car at Willow Brook Fire & Rescue

Station, and there was a tapping on the window. Glancing sideways, I saw Phoebe and Susannah smiling at me.

"Oh, hey, what's up?" I asked as I rolled down the window.

"Come with us," Phoebe said.

"Uh, where?"

"Wildlands, for dinner. Girls only," Susannah replied.

"Okay. What time?"

"Now," Phoebe said, her eyebrows hitching up.

"All right. I'll meet you over there."

I didn't really need to drive over, but I did since it would be dark by the time we finished dinner. As I walked in, I was worrying over my brother. I had a doer kind of personality, always wanting to solve problems and take action, but I had *no* idea how to fix this situation. I desperately and pointlessly wished he hadn't been lured by the stupid easy money in college. He'd been a partier back in those days. Of the two of us, I'd definitely been the more straitlaced one. I wasn't a prude, but I'd been busy with classes and busy with life.

It had never occurred to me that I could've made a bunch of money dealing drugs in college. I let out a sigh and forcibly kicked my worries to the curb. I was in Alaska. My brother was going wherever he was going, and there really was nothing I could do. All I could hope for was that he somehow stayed safe and got himself out of this. I couldn't help the twinge of guilt, though. I really wanted to dump this on my father so he could somehow fix it, but I had no idea how he could remedy it for my brother.

Once I walked into the restaurant, I scanned the room, and my eyes landed on Phoebe pulling out a chair at a table in the corner. The place was hopping, and I dodged customers as I weaved through the tables.

"Hey," I said once I reached them. "You all beat me here."

Susannah grinned. Once we were seated, a waitress appeared. I ordered a water, and we decided to share some appetizers. Once the waitress left, Phoebe glanced over at me, commenting, "I noticed you haven't been drooling over Russell, but he's still staring at your ass."

I rolled my eyes. "Are you serious?"

Phoebe shrugged lightly. "We can only expect so much. I think he's trying to keep it in check. Except that whenever he looks at you, he's all smoldery."

"Absolutely." Susannah nodded emphatically.

"He got all stressed out the other day when we were on a call," Phoebe added.

"He did?"

She nodded slowly. "Yeah. You were ahead on the trail, and the wind was up during the helicopter landing."

I blinked at her. "I'm sure he was just generally concerned."

Phoebe eyed me dubiously, and Susannah's brows hitched up.

"What?" I pressed. "You're not on our crew."

"No, but I *was* on a crew with Ward. And trust me, it's better we're not on the same crew."

"Really?"

"Yeah. It's not just a Ward thing. I worry about him when he's out in the field, and I can manage it better if it's not in the moment."

I didn't know what to think. "Hmm," I replied vaguely, relieved when the waitress appeared to deliver our drinks and assure us our appetizers would be out soon.

Another distraction appeared when Susannah waved at a woman I didn't recognize when she approached the table. I didn't need for the conversation to dwell on Russell and me. I was getting tired of thinking about him, and I was definitely in over my head. My ability to manage my expectations as I'd hoped was limited.

Susannah stood from the table as soon as the woman reached us. "Hey!" She gave the woman a big hug. "How are you? It's been a minute since I saw you."

"It's been a few years," the woman offered with a wry smile.

"I heard about your grandmother," Susannah said. "I'm sorry."

"Thanks," the woman replied. "I'm hoping she turns this around, but it's hard to tell."

Susannah's smile was warm. "How long will you be here?"

"A few weeks."

"Are you meeting anyone here tonight?" Susannah asked. When the woman shook her head, Susannah added, "Do you want to join us?"

"Sure. I mean, if it's okay." The woman glanced at us.

Susannah turned, gesturing from the woman toward us. "This is Mae Townsend. You remember Phoebe, right?"

Mae smiled. "Of course! I didn't see you there."

Phoebe had been looking at something on her phone and finally glanced up. "Oh! Hey!" She stood and hugged Mae as well.

Susannah gestured to me. "This is Paisley. She's a firefighter."

Mae smiled warmly. "I grew up here but then moved away for college and never made it back. Are you sure you don't mind me joining you?"

"Of course not. We have an extra chair anyway. Have a seat." I patted the chair beside me.

Mae was pretty with honey-gold hair and big blue eyes. She slipped into the chair and shrugged out of her jacket. "Well, this place feels exactly the same," she commented as Susannah rounded the table and took the seat across from her.

"It hasn't changed much," Phoebe offered. "They have updated the menu, though."

"And added another wing to the hotel," Susannah chimed in.

Mae laughed softly. "Willow Brook seems like it's growing up."

"Sort of, but not really," Susannah returned. "We have a new pizza place and an art gallery."

"Ooh! We're getting high class," Mae teased. "So you were in Seattle, right?"

Phoebe nodded. "Yup, stayed there after college, but it's good to be back in Alaska."

"It's definitely a change of pace from Seattle," Mae replied.

Phoebe grinned. "For sure. If I need my city dose, I can go to Anchorage."

Mae glanced at me. "Where are you from?"

"I'm from a small town in Washington in the foothills of the Cascades."

Mae's gaze shifted between us. "Three firefighters. Wow. It makes me feel like I'm not that tough."

Susannah rolled her eyes. "You're plenty tough,

Mae." She glanced at me. "She was a sports star in high school."

"What did you do?"

"Cross-country. I ran and ran and ran and got a scholarship to a university in North Carolina, so I took it. Everything was covered, so it was a sweet deal for me," Mae explained.

"There's a guy on our crew from North Carolina," I chimed in.

Mae's gaze sharpened as she glanced in my direction. "Really? Who?"

"Rowan, Rowan Cole," I replied.

"You're kidding me," she said flatly.

"What? You know him?" Phoebe interjected.

Mae let out a heartfelt sigh. "Yes, I do."

"It sounds like there's a story there. What's the scoop?" Susannah asked just as our waitress arrived.

She delivered our appetizers and took Mae's drink order before whisking off to another table. "Help yourself," I said as I doled out the stack of plates the waitress had left for us.

"You sure?" Mae asked.

"Of course," Susannah chirped. "Now, what's the deal with you and Rowan? He seems like a nice enough guy. I'm not on his crew, but Phoebe and Paisley are."

I nodded. "Rowan's a solid guy, kind of quiet."

Phoebe offered, "He's got the whole tall, dark, and mysterious vibe going strong."

Mae pressed her lips together. "We briefly dated in college. It didn't work out," she said curtly. "I can't freaking believe he's here in Willow Brook. What are the chances of that?"

Susannah drummed her fingertips on the table, casting Mae a sympathetic look. "His cousin Lucas is friends with Remy Martin, who's a firefighter here. He told Rowan about the job. Alex Blake is also engaged to Delilah Taylor, who's from the same town."

"You mean Alex of Alex and Holly, the twins?" Mae asked.

"That's the one," Susannah replied.

"Wow. Alex Blake is engaged. I can't believe it."

"He's totally in love with Delilah," Phoebe offered. "And Holly is married to Nate Fox."

Mae's eyes got big. "You are freaking kidding me."

"Nope. Definitely not kidding," Susannah said. "There's a ton more gossip for you to catch up on."

"Have I met these people?" I asked.

"If you haven't, you will. Holly's a nurse at the hospital, and she's awesome. Nate does flights for the firefighter crews in the summer, and Alex is a plane mechanic," Phoebe explained.

Mae popped a halibut bite in her mouth, letting out a satisfied sigh. "God, I missed halibut," she said after she finished chewing. She looked around the restaurant." I hope I don't run into Rowan while I'm here."

Phoebe piped up, "Don't look now, but Rowan just came in with Russell."

"Russell Dane?"

"That's the one," Phoebe replied.

"We're friends. I need to say hi to him," Mae said as she twisted in her chair.

"Why don't you say hi to Russell? I'll avoid him and occupy Rowan for a minute," I offered.

"Oh, you're avoiding Russell?" Mae asked, her gaze curious.

I shrugged, hoping the heat I felt in my cheeks didn't show. "No, not really."

"They're roommates, and they're getting it on, but

they think it's a secret, and Russell won't stop giving her smoldering looks at work. It's a problem." Phoebe's summary was brutally honest.

I glared at her. "Do you have to be that blunt?"

"I'm all about the truth," she said with a shrug.

"Rowan's headed right this way," Susannah warned.

Mae sighed. I was beyond relieved that Mae was here, if only because it helped me feel less insane. The guys came over, and Rowan appeared surprised to see Mae. The tension crackled in the air between them. Mae's blue eyes were glacially cool when she nodded in his direction, then she gave Russell an enthusiastic welcome with a big hug.

"I'm sorry about your grandmother," Russell offered when he stepped back.

"Thank you. She's hanging in there, but I don't think it will be much longer," Mae said with a twist of her lips.

Russell nodded, squeezing her shoulder when she sat down. "Well, we're going to grab a table with the guys. Good to see you all."

As he turned away, Russell's eyes landed on mine. Just a passing glance was enough to scorch me. My skin prickled with heat. Susannah commented, "Smoldering, that's what that was."

I threw a glare in her direction.

## Chapter Twenty-Six
# RUSSELL

"What the hell was that about?" I asked once we were seated.

Rowan had already picked up the menu and didn't even answer. Chase, who'd arrived before us, glanced from him to me, shrugging lightly. "No clue."

"You know Mae Townsend?" I asked.

Rowan looked up from his menu, wincing slightly. "I do."

"How do you know her? She didn't seem happy to see you," I replied.

"Right. Look, I don't actually know what happened. We were really good friends for a few years in college, and then we went on a few dates. She iced me out completely after that, and I never figured out what happened."

"Did you know she was from Willow Brook when you took a job here?" I pressed.

Rowan winced again. "Uh, yeah. Although I didn't even know she lived here. Last I knew, she was still in North Carolina."

I absorbed that. "Hmm, well, she's a friend."

Rowan nodded. "I swear I have no idea why she hates me. If you need to punch me, can we at least take it outside?"

Chase chuckled. "Doesn't seem like that's necessary."

"It's not. Just wondering why she can't stand you," I offered.

"If you find out, let me know," Rowan replied.

A waitress arrived to take our orders, and a few of the other guys showed up. Conversation moved on. I half paid attention, but my mind couldn't resist the detour of Paisley. Hell, she was far more than a detour in my thoughts. She was always there, dancing along the edges when I wasn't distracted. Things were officially complicated enough that Graham saw fit to ask me if something was going on with us today. Apparently, he noticed that I got a little concerned about her during a drop last week. I *had* been concerned, but she'd been fine. I tried to play it off with Graham and told him it was just the usual kind of concern.

Except I hadn't pulled that off. I'd felt his eyes measuring me and assessing. I knew I needed to let Paisley know even though I didn't want to. She was already hypersensitive about the whole thing at work.

---

"Are you kidding me?" Paisley asked. She leaned her elbows on the counter and pressed the heels of her palms into her eyes. When she lifted her head again, she looked more than annoyed. She said something under her breath.

"What?" I prompted.

"Phoebe noticed that you were worried. You know, I can handle myself in the field." She lifted her chin.

"I know you can. You're one of the best on our crew."

"We said this couldn't get complicated," Paisley said, her voice low.

"I know we did. It's not complicated," I insisted, lying through my teeth.

I resorted to playing it off because I didn't know what else to say right now. I sure as hell didn't know what to do about my feelings. All of my efforts to keep things compartmentalized and uncomplicated weren't working. I kept remembering my father, remembering how devastated my mother had been when he died, and remembering the day I showed up at the rescue. Fuck.

"Maybe we should—" She began talking, but I shook my head sharply. "You don't even know what I was going to say."

"Okay, fine. What were you about to say?"

"Maybe we should stop."

"Stop what?" I knew what she meant, but I preferred to play stupid.

She took a deep breath. "What we're doing. Actually, what *are* we doing?" she pressed.

"Having a good time." I tried to keep my tone light. "It's kept us from arguing at work."

"But maybe we've gotten rid of the tension, and we're friends now," she said, her voice sounding strained.

"The tension hasn't gone anywhere," I said flatly. "Do you think it has?"

We stared at each other. I thought for a minute she was going to try to lie about it, but she didn't. She shook her head slowly back and forth as pink stained her cheeks. "No." The single word was a raspy whisper and sent a sizzle of heat through me.

I didn't realize my hands were gripping the countertop until I released them. I walked in a circle and opened the refrigerator for no reason before turning back to face her.

"Hungry?" she asked, her brows hitching up. I shook my head. "We have to be able to work together, Russell."

"I know," I said quickly. "I haven't been staring at your ass." Another lie for the books, but I thought that was more of the white-lie variety. No big deal. *Bullshit.*

Paisley laughed softly. "According to Phoebe, you give me smoldery looks."

I chuckled. "Ah, perhaps so. Apparently, I need to keep it together better at work."

"It's not like it's really been a problem," she offered.

It almost annoyed me that she was more contained than me at work. But knowing how she kept everything so tight around her brother, I supposed that made sense. I was falling for her and getting in over my head while she was busy keeping her distance. I knew it wasn't just me. I knew how it felt when we were together, but none of that mattered right now. My resolve to tell her about Graham's concern was waning. I forced myself to do it, though.

"Graham might've noticed something."

"What?" she squeaked.

"Probably that I was worried about you out in the field. I told him it was nothing, and I think he bought it." Actually, I was pretty sure he didn't, but I wasn't about to fess up to that.

I did the only thing I could think to do and rounded the counter, resting my hands on either side of her. She spun around on the stool and peered up at me. "Maybe we should—"

"Do this," I said, dipping my head and fitting my mouth over hers. Our kiss flashed into a bonfire. She flexed into me, letting out a little moan. This was the one thing we did *really* well.

Maybe not the only thing, but at least I could forget about everything else while I lost myself in Paisley. In a hot second, we were tugging at each other's clothes, and I was lifting her in my arms as she curled her legs around my waist. I carried her upstairs to her bed.

I loved everything about her—the feel of her nipples ruching under my touch, her belly trembling when I dropped hot kisses over it, her channel convulsing around me as I sank my thick shaft inside. She shuddered roughly around me. With each surge into her silky slick core, I watched as her eyes darkened and my own release yanked me over the edge. Falling asleep beside her came easy as darkness cloaked us.

## Chapter Twenty-Seven
# PAISLEY

I didn't tell Russell my plan. The following morning, we showered together like we usually did. He pinned me against the tiled wall, and I savored every second of it. I'd tried to keep my heart tucked away behind a sturdy door—setting the lock firmly. But *he* was the key, and he'd rattled it loose. I couldn't figure out how to close the bolt again.

Even if my heart was a goner, I still needed to be smart. I didn't want to lose people's respect at work. I'd made a decision. I knew there was an opening on one of the other crews. I hoped Graham would understand. Since he had said something to Russell, I decided to be honest with him. That was the easiest option. I went into the station early because Graham was almost always there. Maisie was on the phone in the front and waved to me when I passed by.

I peered into the office Graham shared with the other crew superintendents, relieved to discover he was the only one there. "Morning," he said.

"You happen to have a few minutes to talk?" I asked.

"Of course, come on in."

I stepped in and closed the door behind me. His brows lifted when he noticed that detail, but he didn't comment on it. I sat down across from his desk. He closed his laptop and lifted his cup of coffee. It was a red cup with a distinctive drawing of the old fire station on it.

My stomach felt tight, and I was way too nervous. I began, "So, uh ..." Only two words in, and I didn't know how to explain myself. I bit my lip.

"Paisley, you okay?" Graham asked, his eyes warm.

My fingers were laced together in my lap, and I clenched them tightly. "Maybe, uh ... Look, I know I haven't been here that long, but I was wondering what you thought about me switching to Ward's crew?" Graham remained quiet, and I forged ahead. "Russell mentioned that you spoke to him about worrying about me. I don't want there to be tension, or things to be weird."

Graham looked at me quietly for a long moment before his head dipped in a nod. "Has something happened, or has Russell done something that I need to be concerned about?"

"Absolutely not," I said firmly.

My cheeks were burning, and I closed my eyes, feeling mortified.

"You don't have to tell me the whole story, but I have noticed some tension between you two. If you think that's the best option, then I support it." My eyes flew wide. "We have a full crew now, so you shifting over to Ward's crew is easily managed. The timing's good since we're heading into winter."

Relief whooshed through me. "Thank you. Should I talk to Ward first?"

A light knock sounded on the door, followed by Ward's voice. "Can I come in?"

Graham flashed me a grin. "Good timing. It helps that we share this space." He called, "Come on in."

Ward stepped into the room, glancing back and forth between us. Graham jumped right in. "Paisley was just asking me about shifting over to your crew."

"Seriously?" Ward asked with a grin.

He could be kind of an intimidating guy, but the second he smiled, all intimidation dissipated. Tall with dark hair and silver eyes, he was handsome and fit as all hotshots were.

"I've heard you're rock solid. If you want to switch to my crew, the job is yours."

"Oh, that would be great."

Graham divided a glance between us. "How about you finish out the week on our rotation and then switch over to his crew next week?"

Ward sat down beside me. "Anything I need to know?"

"Not a thing," Graham said easily.

I sure as hell didn't want Ward to get any hint about me getting tangled up with Russell. Earning respect as a woman on a hotshot crew was no easy feat, and if the other guys thought I was screwing around, it wouldn't help me at all. I was relieved when Graham's cell phone rang, and he stood to leave the room. That relief disappeared the second Ward spoke.

"Susannah mentioned something about you and Russell." I opened my mouth and shut it when he continued. "No need to explain. She and I were on a crew together, and now we're married, and we have a kid. If anyone understands this kind of thing, I do. It's not great for there to be that kind of complication on a crew, though. Absolutely no judgment from me. Does Russell know you asked about this?"

I shook my head. "We're not getting married, and we don't have a kid."

Ward's eyes skated over my face, and I worried he saw way too much. He shrugged. "Ah, okay. I won't say anything until the rest of your crew knows about the move. As Graham suggested, you can start with our rotation next week. I'll send you an email with the schedule. We're headed into winter, so it'll be slower."

"Thank you for understanding," I managed.

"You got it." Ward stood, clapping me on the shoulder as he did.

I left the office with my stomach still tied in knots because now I had to let Russell and the rest of my crew know.

## Chapter Twenty-Eight
# RUSSELL

"What?"

Graham eyed me. "Yeah, Paisley'll switch rotations next week. Thought you might want to know up front. She hasn't talked to you about it?"

"No," I said curtly. "This is bullshit."

"Actually, I think it's for the best."

"Why?" I practically barked back at Graham.

He stepped past me and closed the door to the office. Resting his hips against the desk, he gave me a long, considering look. "Dude, I've known you for so long I don't remember not knowing you."

"What the fuck does that have to do with this?" I muttered.

"I think you have more than just casual feelings for Paisley. At the interview, you were kind of an ass about it, but I think then it was just lust."

I opened my mouth to argue, and his brows hitched up, almost daring me. I let out a sigh. "But we got past that," I said, feeling way more defensive than I preferred.

"Yeah, that's great, but now you're dealing with this thing called feelings."

"It's—"

"Complicated," he filled in for me. "No matter what, it *is* best for the crew and for you and for her to handle it this way. Hell, that's what Susannah and Ward did, and it was a smart move. Respect is hard enough for women to earn as hotshots. Things can get messy. Ward's pretty open about why it turned out best for Susannah and him not to be on the same crew. If you two don't work things out, well then..." Graham let his words trail off.

"That'll be even more complicated," I grumbled and then practically bit my tongue off because I was about to say that wasn't an option.

"You're not going to like the other thing I have to say," Graham added.

"What's that?" I was feeling downright sullen now.

"You have been off a hair, not at work, but personally, ever since what happened with your dad."

"Graham," I warned.

He didn't heed me. "I'm your friend, so I'm saying something. I think it hit you hard, and I get it. You don't even talk about it. Hell, I don't even think you let yourself think about it. Since he passed, you've been different."

Graham couldn't have known how spot-on he was because that was the plain truth. Every time my mind went in the direction of my father, I just shut it down. My chest hurt and my throat ached, and fuck it all, I was not going to burst into tears, not at work. I wasn't one of those assholes who didn't think men should cry, but I needed to have some dignity.

I breathed in slowly, keeping my eyes trained on the tile lines a few feet beyond the desk. After several deep breaths, I leveled my gaze with Graham's and nodded. "I know. It was hard, and I miss him."

"Of course, you do."

"You're bringing this up now, why?"

Graham cast me a rueful smile, the understanding in his eyes making my chest hurt all over again. "I'm not really sure. Somehow, my brain thinks your feelings for Paisley and maybe how you got a little overprotective out in the field the other day are somehow tied to your dad. But what the hell do I know? I'm just a guy."

My laugh was dry, and even I could hear the bitterness in it. "You're not just some guy. You're a friend who I've known for as long as I can remember. You're also a kick-ass dad, and you might have a little more knowledge about relationships than I do."

Graham shrugged, casting me a lopsided grin. "Maybe a few months of knowledge, but that's it."

We laughed together. "You going to be okay?" he asked after we stood there silently for probably too long.

I nodded. "Yeah. Thanks for the heads-up on the crew change for Paisley."

"You want to go grab a beer?"

"Nah, not up for that tonight, but thanks."

My friend nodded. "Okay. I'll see you at work tomorrow."

After leaving the office, I walked down the hallway to the reception area, and my eyes landed on the giant pumpkin full of candy perched on Maisie's desk. She was on the phone. Normally, I would have wanted to stop and steal some of that candy, but I wasn't in the mood. I drove toward home, not even sure that was where I wanted to go. I felt pulled in two directions.

Graham's observations had me partially wanting to

run from Paisley. Maybe it was best she wasn't on my crew. But now, I'd have to worry about her even more because she would be out in the field without me. Of course, that only proved Graham's point. I didn't know what the hell to think about his observation about my dad.

I took a sharp turn before I got to the lake house, driving down a narrow road that spit me out at a secluded parking area on the lake. It wasn't frequented by many, except for high school kids looking for a private place to make out. For now, no one was here.

I parked and stared out over the lake. I missed my dad so much. He died after his gear broke, and that sucked. My dad had loved the outdoors. That was how my parents ended up here. He came up here for some temporary summer job, and they stayed. He wasn't even working the day the accident happened. He'd gone climbing, and something went wrong. His harness broke, and he died.

By the time I got there with the crew, he was already dead. I kept replaying it as if I could've done something to change the series of events, which was crazy thinking. I took a breath, watching as a flock of trumpeter swans floated serenely on the water. The sun was setting, and the lake was awash in a shimmer of pink and lavender. Sunsets in autumn in Alaska were glorious. I suppose that could be said about any time of year, but I loved the colors in the fall.

When the moon came to claim the sky from the sun, I breathed in a gulp of air, letting it out in a rush. "I miss you, Dad," I whispered into the truck.

We'd fished here many times when I was a kid. I didn't catch much, but it was where I learned to fish and always had fun. When I got older, we fished on the inlet in boats and went dipnetting during the summer. I climbed out of my truck, idly kicking a loose pebble as I crossed the gravel to stand at the edge of the water. The tall summer grasses were dying and were bleached. A raven called with another answering in return.

That awful feeling I'd started to get in Graham's office finally began to abate. I'd wanted a chance to say goodbye to my dad, and he'd given it to me in a small way. Even though I was pissed about it, it probably *was* best for Paisley to switch crews because I couldn't seem to keep my hands off her. And I knew I was in love with her. That awareness hit me like a gong reverberating in my chest—again and again and again.

Holy shit. I swallowed and took another breath. Things really were complicated. So much for no strings. I knew what I felt when I was with Paisley alone at night. But damn, that woman played her cards so close to her chest that I didn't know if she'd ever face her feelings.

I gave my head a shake, chuckling as I turned away. In a way, I felt lighter, if only because Graham forced me to admit something. The weight of loving Paisley wasn't heavy, but it was uncertain. I didn't know what to do with it.

I climbed in my truck and drove home, almost surprised to see her car there. She was a master of avoidance. I suppose I recognized that tendency because, in a way, I was myself or had been in certain areas of my life. I walked into the house to find her in the kitchen staring in the pantry.

My heart turned over in my chest, and warmth filled the space. She was always at a loss in the kitchen unless there was something in a box. Even then, I could feel her resigned to the decision because she felt as if it was her only option.

"I'll cook dinner," I called as I shrugged out of my jacket and kicked my boots off by the door.

Paisley's eyes tracked me as I crossed the kitchen. I got angry all over again. I stopped a few feet away, tossing my keys in the bowl on the table by the counter. The clatter of them landing was loud in the quiet space.

"Why didn't you tell me?" I asked.

She bit her lip. "I don't know. I guess I was worried you'd be upset."

"Well, I'm upset you didn't tell me."

She stared at me. "What?" she pressed when I didn't say anything further.

"So, it's okay to spend every night with me, but I'm not even worth a conversation that you asked to switch crews? I'm assuming you asked because of me."

The brief respite of peace I'd found only moments earlier had gone up in smoke. I was hurt and angry, and it was because I'd gone and fallen in love with her. Like a dumbass.

"Russell." She shook her head quickly. "I don't know how to explain, and I didn't want to have an argument about it." She gestured back and forth between us. "*This* is what I didn't want to do."

"But you want to do this?" In a flash, I was standing in front of her, one arm curling around her waist as I pulled her fast against me.

The minute our mouths met, it felt like a flame racing up to the end of a fuse and catching a gust of wind, making it burn fast. Our kiss was a tangle, our teeth clanking together at one point.

Then it was like it always was with her. I couldn't get enough, and she met me every step of the way— her tongue dueling with mine, her hands impatient on my body, her palm curling around my cock, teasing me while I muttered filthy endearments.

Because I lost my mind when I was with her, and the fire took over, sizzling through my veins, I had her right there in the kitchen again. This time, her legs were curled around my hips as I lifted her onto the counter.

When I sank into her, seating myself deeply, I held still, murmuring, "Paisley, look at me."

Her lashes lifted slowly, and her heavy-lidded gaze met mine. I could feel the echoing beat of her heart against my chest. Her nipples were drawn into taut peaks, pressed against me. The core of her was slick with arousal and rippling around me. The sound of our breathing filled the space around us as we stared at each other. I sensed the moment she wanted to look away, the moment the intimacy became just too much.

But she didn't. She lifted her chin and blinked. For a second, I could've sworn I saw the sheen of tears in her eyes, but then one of her heels spurred my ass, and she said, "More."

I could only give her what she wanted. What she wanted was what I wanted. I drew back and thrust into her again, holding her fast until she flew apart in my arms, her entire body trembling as she pulled my own release from me. Once again, I carried her to bed. This time, to mine.

It wasn't until the following morning that I realized my mistake.

## Chapter Twenty-Nine
## PAISLEY

Russell was still sound asleep when I slipped quietly out of bed before the sun came up. Oh, my God, it was difficult to force myself to get out of that bed. I was toasty warm and had my knee curled over one of his thighs with my palm on his chest. I could feel his heart beating under my touch, and his breathing came in the slow, even rhythm of sleep. I took a moment to soak in the shadowy lines of his face and let my hand trail over his abdomen as I drew away.

Though I risked waking him up, I was feeling greedy and already bereft at my decision. I was in *waaaay* too deep. I didn't know what Russell wanted, but I wasn't ready to figure it out for myself. With my worry about my brother heavy in my heart, I knew I needed to go back to Washington and straighten things out.

I'd already booked a flight, but first, I needed to create some space. Madison had said I could stay in her spare bedroom. I tiptoed upstairs, not daring to go into the kitchen. It was directly above Russell's bedroom, and I didn't want to run the risk of him hearing my footsteps. I tiptoed all the way upstairs and quickly packed. Fortunately, I didn't have much. Russell didn't know I'd done the laundry yesterday and even left the sheets clean.

I'd already written a note to leave for him and placed it on the kitchen counter. I wasn't completely running away. He would see me around, but we needed some space, like a few thousand miles. I'd have to make do with the amount of distance created by not falling into his arms every night.

He would be pissed, and maybe he had a right to that. We'd said no strings, and I was tied up in emotional knots with far too many threads leading to him. I just didn't know what I wanted.

If he knew what I'd been covering up for my brother, he would be horrified. *I* was horrified. I'd already fielded two phone calls from my parents in the past few days, worried about my brother's vacation and lack of communication. By the time I reached Madison's house, the sun was rising. She'd told me she was over at Graham's and to let myself in.

I was profoundly grateful for her offer. I didn't even think I could call her a close friend yet, but when she saw me yesterday, she said she understood the need for a fresh start. She'd told me a safe place to land was always a good thing. She'd also told me that Graham thought Russell was in love with me, which freaked me right the hell out.

I was pretty sure I was in love with him, but I was dealing with a mess, and I needed to clean it up first. At least then, I could be honest with him. I'd planned ahead. I even had some groceries. Madison had left a note on the counter, telling me where to find the coffee and such, so I decided to help myself. I didn't have the nerve to go to Firehouse Café this morning because I didn't want to run into Russell.

As I sipped my coffee, guilt and uncertainty began to swamp me. Maybe this wasn't the best way to handle it. *You don't even know what you want right now. You need to go and deal with this mess with Ryder.*

One thing at a time. *Maybe things will work out with Russell, but if he knew you were deep into a yearslong lie involving your brother's serious crimes, he might reconsider.*

I sighed. My throat felt tight, and I was so pissed off and disappointed with my brother. I had just finished my first cup of coffee, which was a relief because that was when I got the first text.

Russell: *Seriously? You couldn't, at least, have the nerve to talk to me face-to-face? Why are you running from me?*

I swiped the tears from my cheeks.

Me: *I'm not running from you. I have some things to deal with. I promise we'll talk when that's done.*

Russell: *Are you planning to work next week?*

Me: *I'm not sure.*

After my meeting with Ward, I'd checked with Graham and him about taking a week between my transition to the new crew.

My reply was met with complete silence. I so desperately wanted to call him or run back to the house and explain. I knew I should've scrounged up the courage to tell him my plans last night, but I'd let the fire burning between us consume me instead.

Ugh. I poured myself another cup of coffee, startled when there was a knock on the door. Madison had assured me Graham would not tell Russell I was over here. I tiptoed out to the entryway to see Madison peering in through one of the windows flanking the door with a cheerful corgi smiling through the other.

"You can come in, you know. It's your house," I said as I swung open the door.

She smiled. "I know, but I didn't want to startle you. You said you were coming over early."

Closing the door behind her, I sighed. "Yeah."

"What happened? Did you sneak out on Russell?" I looked at her, nodding slowly. She walked past me. "Did you make some coffee?"

"Yes."

"Is there enough for me?"

"Of course." Her corgi trotted along with her, pausing to sniff at my ankles.

I scratched behind his ears. I'd met him before when she stopped by the station with him.

"Wilbur's looking smart today." I watched as his alert gaze scanned the area before he followed her into the kitchen.

Madison chuckled while she poured herself a cup of coffee. "He *is* smart." She took a swallow of coffee before sitting down at the table across from me. "All right, I know we're not besties yet, but I'm committed to making friends. What the hell is going on, and why would you sneak out like that?"

"I think I'm a coward," I offered.

The next thing I knew, I told Madison the whole story, ending with the most obvious conclusion, "It wasn't supposed to get complicated."

She nodded slowly. "It never is. It wasn't supposed to get complicated for Graham and me either. I mean, he's got a teenage daughter. My plans didn't include getting involved with anyone, much less a father."

"You two seem to be doing well."

"I think so. We're figuring it out. Honestly, all I have to say is this. If you didn't have real feelings for

Russell, you wouldn't have felt the need to sneak out. Maybe you should think about what that means."

My eyes narrowed, and Madison cocked her head to the side, giving a slight shrug. "I'm just sayin'. I'm no expert on romance, trust me, but feelings are feelings. If you didn't have any, you probably would've told him you were leaving instead of sneaking out."

I let out a groan and took a long swallow of coffee. "Fine. You may have a point."

Her smile was warm and understanding. "Maybe, maybe not. You're not going to be able to avoid him for too long, though." When I rolled my eyes, Madison's look was knowing. "This town is small, and you work with him. Maybe you have a week off, but let's get real."

Madison left to go to Anchorage for work after assuring me to treat the place like my own. She asked me to take Wilbur out a few times during the day. Her little dog seemed content to curl up beside me while I sat on the couch, staring aimlessly out the windows. For the first time ever, I wished I had a regular job where I needed to check email or call someone.

When you were off duty as a hotshot firefighter, there was literally nothing to do. I didn't dare go into the station because that would mean running into Russell. As it was, I was feeling more foolish by the minute about my plan. I *had* needed the time off, and I definitely needed to put some space between us. But Madison's points about my feelings—stupid feelings—had me feeling even more cowardly.

Feeling restless, I stood and walked into the guest bedroom to fetch my cell phone and laptop computer. I had a few bills to pay online, so I figured I might as well take care of that. I had my bills paid inside of fifteen minutes. I was feeling absolutely ridiculous that

I was paying rent to Russell's mother through the little online pay portal when I didn't even know if I was going to return. I thought maybe once he knew what I'd been hiding, he'd think I wasn't the person he thought I was. Keeping my brother's secrets made me feel like a fraud about everything.

I put my laptop away and resumed looking out the windows. Madison had a sweet view into the trees with the mountains in the distance. She'd mentioned she and Graham hadn't settled on where they planned to live together long-term, and I thought she should tell Graham to move here. Although I'd bet he had a great view too.

I flushed all over out of embarrassment. Graham knew about Russell and me. He didn't seem to think less of me because of it, although it spoke volumes that he thought it was wise for me to switch crews.

Russell had stopped texting me, and I was torn between relief and disappointment. That made me feel ridiculous. I almost jumped out of my skin when my phone rang. I eyed my phone where it sat on the coffee table. Leaning forward, I saw it was my parents' number.

I dreaded when my parents called. I'd already been keeping secrets for my brother, but it was exhausting. I tried to tell myself my brother was on vacation, which was true. But that didn't change the fact that I wasn't telling them the whole truth and hadn't been for over a year. They would be heartbroken.

With a sigh, I reached for the phone and slid my thumb across the screen. "Hey, Mom or Dad," I answered.

"Well, hello, Paisley," my father said. "I wasn't sure if you'd be out in the wilderness today."

"No, not today," I replied lightly. Of course, that

*was* true. But it felt as if I was hiding yet another thing from my parents. Not that it was any of their business that I had a hot-roommates-with-benefits thing going on with Russell that was getting way too freaking complicated. I wasn't about to fess up to taking a week off to screw my head on straight.

"How's it going, Dad?" I asked, injecting cheerfulness into my tone.

"Well, I wanted to check in with you when your mother wasn't around."

I moaned silently. "Is everything okay?"

"Ah, depends on what you mean by okay."

"Dad, just tell me what's going on."

"I'll cut to the chase. I'm concerned your brother is involved in one of my investigations. I suspect he is on vacation but not for innocuous reasons."

My eyes stung with tears, and a lump lodged in my throat. I sent up a silent apology to my brother and took a deep breath. "I think you're onto something, Dad."

He went completely silent, and I could've sworn he was holding his breath. After a long moment, he let out a ragged sigh. "What do you know, Paisley?"

"He's in over his head, and I'm tired of worrying about him." That wasn't *all* I knew. But it was all I was willing to tell my father.

"I'm handing the case over to someone else because I can't be working on it if your brother's involved. If you talk to him, let him know that they are willing to cut him a deal if he's willing to testify."

"Are you serious?" I heard myself asking.

"Completely, and that's all I know. I can't help him any more than that. I think it's best if he doesn't hear that from me. The lead prosecutor gave me permission to tell him, but I haven't had a chance to speak with him. He's been calling periodically, but it's usually when your mother's home. I sense you've been trying to protect us as much as your brother. I'd prefer not to tell your mother until we know what will happen with your brother. This will send her into a tailspin, and I'd rather not do that."

Suddenly, tears were rolling down my cheeks, and I took a shuddering breath. "You okay there, Paisley?" my father asked.

"No and yes. Dad, I'm sorry."

"For what? Keeping your brother's secrets? I don't know if he asked you to, but I understand why you made that choice. Don't beat yourself up. Let's just hope he makes the smart choice now. Please let me know if you hear from him."

I sniffled, dragging my sleeve across my nose. "I will, Dad. I love you."

After we ended the call, I sat there with my phone in hand, wondering what to do. I didn't even know how to call my brother because he said he would be using burner phones. "You idiot," I muttered to myself. Unblocking him would do me no good at this point.

I sighed and tossed my phone on the couch cushions. Standing, I curled my arms around my waist and strode to the windows, pacing back and forth in a short path. Wilbur watched me calmly, his brown eyes blinking every time I looked his way.

"I'm not that ridiculous," I said to him. He blinked again. I realized abruptly that I didn't want to stay here this week. I called the airport and changed my flight to Seattle. I had a hunch I knew where my brother was.

After that, I texted Madison, telling her I was leaving for now.

Madison: *Are you okay?*

Me: *I'm fine. I'm going to use the week to go visit my family.*

That was completely true, but I was getting sick of half-truths. She assured me she'd be back in a few hours to pick up Wilbur. After taking Wilbur out for a walk, I made sure he had fresh water and then got ready to go.

I hesitated to text Russell, but I forced myself to muster up some courage.

Me: *If my brother calls by chance, can you tell him to call my cell phone? Please. I promise we'll talk soon.*

## Chapter Thirty
# RUSSELL

"What do you mean?"

Maisie looked across her desk. "She's off," she repeated. "You didn't know?"

Just then, Graham's girlfriend, Madison, came walking through the front doors to the station. "Do you know for how long?" I asked.

Maisie pressed her lips together before letting out a sharp sigh. "No, I don't. I do keep on top of everything, but I didn't catch that detail. All I know is she took the week off between switching crews."

Madison stopped beside the desk, her eyes landing on mine. "She went to visit her family. You didn't know?"

Fuck my life. I was getting tired of not knowing what the hell was going on. "No, but how do *you* know?"

I felt like I knew Paisley better than Madison, at least. We *had* been pretty up close and personal. "She was staying at my place, but she texted me this morning and said she was going to Seattle to see her family."

I had so many freaking questions, and I couldn't ask a single one. Meanwhile, Maisie and Madison were staring at me avidly. "Wow, thanks for the update," I said before turning on my heel and shouldering through the swinging door into the back hallway. I was looking at the floor and promptly collided with someone. "Oh, sorry."

Glancing up, I found Rowan standing in front of me. He shrugged. "No worries." He gave me a curious look. "Are you okay?"

"Yeah, I'm fine," I muttered.

"You sure don't seem fine. Do you need anything?" he pressed.

I sighed, leaning against the wall and bouncing one of my boot heels against it. "Paisley switched crews."

"Yeah, I heard," he said slowly. "You're not cool with that? You weren't thrilled with her when she started, although you seemed to change your tune."

"Fuck," I mumbled.

"You could just fess up to it and deal," he commented.

I gave him a sharp look. "Fess up to what?"

"Dude, you've got it bad for her."

Maybe I didn't know Rowan well, but I already knew him to be an honest and direct guy. He tended to be on the quiet side, but when he spoke, it was clear and to the point.

"Is it that obvious?"

"Yes, it's *that* obvious," he said with a slight grin.

I leaned my head back, thumping it against the wall. "I'm a dumbass."

"Hey, I've been stupid too," he offered. "Sometimes, men are stupid at the worst possible times."

I pushed away from the wall. Clapping him on the

shoulder, I nodded. "You're right on that. Catch you later."

I missed Paisley so much it hurt, and I felt like an idiot. I also felt like she'd been holding something back. All of it circled back to her brother. I only hoped maybe if she was going to see him, she would finally straighten that out. In the meantime, all I could do was wait. And fucking miss her.

---

That very evening, the house phone rang. I stared at it like it was a grenade about to explode. Stalking across the kitchen, I lifted the receiver quickly.

"Hello?"

"Hey, Russell, it's Ryder. Is Paisley around?"

"No. As far as I understand, she went down to visit her family."

"You're fucking kidding me," he muttered.

"Nope, definitely wouldn't kid about that. How come you don't know?"

"Because I'm a fucking asshole," he said flatly.

"I appreciate the honesty. So, obviously you're not there then?"

"No, I'm not. I'm in Anchorage at the airport."

"What? You didn't let her know you were coming to visit?"

"Obviously not," her brother countered quickly.

"You need a ride?"

"Nah, I already have a rental. Mind if I crash in her room?"

I turned that idea over in my thoughts before replying, "Fine by me." I planned to take advantage of this opportunity to get some answers out of him.

Approximately an hour and a half later, I was

sitting in the kitchen with Ryder. He shared Paisley's coloring, but that was all they had in common.

"What the hell is going on?" I asked when I pushed the pizza box toward him.

Ryder held my gaze for a moment that stretched before he shrugged, almost to himself. "I'm in trouble, and Paisley's been keeping it from our parents. She feels like shit about it."

"She texted me that if you called to ask you to call her cell."

What I thought was guilt flitted through his eyes when he shook his head. "I know she's a much bigger person than me, and I don't want to pull her further into my mess."

"Dude, you came here to see her," I pointed out, annoyed with him.

After finishing a bite of pizza, he said, "I know, but now I know she's down there, so I don't want to make things worse."

"You gonna tell me what the hell is going on?"

"Probably not, but I'm going to call our parents. I'm assuming she's there. Do you know when she left?"

Fuck. This felt weird. I sure as hell didn't want to tell her brother about the tension between us. I didn't know what he saw in my expression, but his eyes narrowed.

"Something's going on between you two," he stated bluntly.

"It's none of your fucking business if there is," I countered swiftly.

"I'm her brother. Of course, it's my fucking business."

I rolled my eyes. "I think Paisley would disagree."

He chuckled dryly, shaking his head as he tore off a bite of pizza. "You're in love with her."

"What?"

I knew I *was* in love with her, but I wasn't about to fess up to him about that. Paisley would fucking kill me. I hadn't even told her.

"I know you're not gonna talk to me about it. I'm just saying. I know the look."

"What look?"

"I've been in love before," he replied.

I rolled my eyes. "Somehow, I doubt that."

"And how would you know?"

"How about we skip this topic?" I returned after a brief stare down with him. I was unsettled and angry with him about whatever mess he'd landed Paisley in. Dwelling on my feelings for her wasn't going to solve anything. "Why don't you go ahead and call your parents?"

"Why is it so important?"

"Because I'd like to know Paisley arrived safe and sound, you asshole."

Ryder's brows hitched up, but he shrugged. We ate in silence, and then her brother finally called their parents. Only seconds after he greeted whoever answered the call, dread settled in a cold ball in my gut.

"What do you mean she's not there?" Her brother pressed his palm into his forehead before glancing over at me. He nodded along to something. "I gotta go. I have an idea where she is, and I'll call you once I sort it out."

"What the fuck is going on?" I asked the second he hung up the phone.

"I think my sister probably thinks she knows where I am. Except I'm not there. I'm here instead. I need to go."

"I'm going with you," I stated flatly.

Ryder opened his mouth to argue, and I laid it on the line. "You're right. I'm in love with Paisley. And I'm fucking pissed at you. I also don't trust you to make sure she's okay. I have a friend who's a pilot. We can probably get a private flight down there faster than any commercial flight." Her brother's eyes widened. "I'm a hotshot firefighter. I know lots of pilots. Let me give my friend a call."

I tried to call Paisley, but she didn't answer. I was torn between fury at her brother and fear that she wasn't safe.

"You mind telling me what the fuck is going on, for real this time?" I asked once we were in my truck, and I was hauling ass down the highway to meet Nate at the airport.

Nate wasn't going to fly us, but he'd gotten us onto a private business flight. Another friend, Alex Blake, was an airplane mechanic, and he knew this flight had room.

"Because I'm a dumbass, I started making money hand over fist in college selling high-end drugs. It's continued to be a good source of income, but now I need to get out. I'm trying to do exactly that," Ryder explained.

"Are you using the product?" I asked sharply.

"Fuck no," he said. "I haven't partied since college. I hardly even drink. I get why you might not believe me, but it's the fucking truth."

I didn't know why, but I believed him. There wasn't even an ounce of defensiveness in his tone. I moved on. "Isn't your father a district attorney or something?" I could've sworn Paisley had mentioned something like that.

As soon as I slid my eyes sideways to meet Ryder's gaze, I knew I was right. "Yeah."

I let out a low whistle. "And Paisley's been carrying the secret for you."

"Dude, she found out by accident. I did *not* burden her."

"You're her brother, and you're doing dangerous shit. She's intensely loyal, so she obviously feels like shit because she's probably keeping it from your parents."

Her brother let out a weary sigh. "I fucking know. Dude, why do you think I'm trying to extricate myself from this situation?"

I shook my head and drove. I tried calling Paisley again before the plane took off. This time, I left her a message that I was with her brother and we were on the way to her.

## Chapter Thirty-One
# PAISLEY

The old summerhouse was dark when my headlights arced across the front of it, illuminating the dormer windows peeking out like eyes in the night. Disappointment settled inside me, churning into the worry that had been chasing its tail in my thoughts.

I was positive my brother might've been here. Okay, maybe not positive, but reasonably confident. We used to spend summers here back when everything seemed easier. Those halcyon days felt a million miles away in the rainy darkness.

I turned off my headlights and left my rental car running because it was cold and raining.

"Where are you?" I muttered into the darkness.

Getting a call from my brother's friend had me deeply worried. The relief I'd felt at realizing my father finally knew what was going on had quickly been washed away. My brother was protecting me more than I'd thought. I hadn't been so foolish to think he told me everything, but I sure hadn't realized one of his best friends was in deep with him.

I fished inside my purse, pulling out the key to this

place. When my parents spent a few weeks here every summer, I usually joined them for a weekend or two. Just as I was about to turn the car engine off and climb out, I saw a glimmer of light through the darkness and realized one of the rooms in the back had a light on. Maybe my brother was here after all. I was a little nervous, but my determination to find Ryder overrode my nerves. I checked my phone to see if there was any reception. Not even a single bar. I turned the engine off and waited for a few more minutes before I climbed out with the key clutched in my hand.

I knew the pathway in the darkness and counted the stone steps. When I was a little girl, I'd run down them in my bare feet to where they curled around the house and led into the trees on one side. My footsteps were quiet. I slid the key into the lock, and it turned smoothly. Opening the door, I called out, "Ryder?"

Silence greeted me. I walked through the living room into the dining area, where a hallway flanked off to one side. Following the light, I hoped it was Ryder here. Alas, it was my brother's friend Todd who'd called me.

"What the hell are you doing here, Paisley?" he asked as he stepped out of the room.

"Looking for my brother. What the hell are you doing here?"

"I was looking for him too."

He curled a hand around my elbow and tugged me into the enclosed glass porch at the back of the house. There was a single lamp on in the corner. "What are you doing here, Todd?"

He sat down in a chair, resting his elbows on his knees and tunneling his hands through his hair. "There's a reason your brother went on vacation."

"I know that. I came down to try to find him."

Todd lifted his head, his eyes going wide. "Are you fucking kidding me?"

"Uh, no." I silently cursed. I'd known Todd since high school and would've trusted him once upon a time. Now, I wasn't so sure.

"You can trust me. Ryder and I are both trying to get out of this mess."

"Well, it's quite the fucking mess," I muttered

"Is your cell working?" Todd asked.

"I doubt it. Reception's not great here." I slipped my phone out of my purse first, checking the screen again. "Still no reception," I muttered to myself.

"There's not great reception, but your parents left the Wi-Fi on."

"They did?"

Todd nodded. "They sure did. Go figure."

I tapped into my settings and selected the network for my parents' place. A minute later, several texts came in, including the banner for a voicemail from Russell. A confusing sense of relief and anticipation shot through me.

"What's up?" Todd asked.

"A friend called, someone I was hoping to hear from," I replied. I wasn't about to get into the mess of my feelings about Russell with him. Yes, he was a friend, and an old friend at that, but discussing romance with my brother and any of his friends wasn't something I cared to do.

Lifting the phone to my ear, I tapped play on the message, making sure the volume was low. "Hey, Paisley. It's Russell. I'm guessing you went to Washington to find your brother, and your brother's here. He is seriously stressing out, so now we're flying down there. Please call me and let me know where you're at. Your best bet is to go to your parents' house. Your brother's kind of panicking. I guess his friend is a problem right now. Please call me when you get this."

Fear shot through me, but I kept my expression neutral. I lowered the phone as I tapped the button to lock the screen.

"Everything okay?" Todd asked.

"Oh, yeah. So, uh, how long are you planning to stay here?"

My mind spun over whether or not Todd was the friend Ryder was concerned about. Surely, Todd wouldn't hurt me. That would be crazy. But then, if he was involved with whatever my brother was doing, it wasn't as if I could assume he was making good choices.

"I'm not sure. I'm trying to get ahold of your brother. He's been using burner phones and turned off his old number."

I nodded slowly. "Well, since Ryder isn't here, I think I'm going to leave. It seems like you're trying to lay low, and you certainly don't need my rental car out front drawing attention here. You might want to keep the light off back here."

Todd narrowed his eyes, and I still didn't know how to interpret anything with him. "Why don't you stay put?" he asked as I turned toward the hallway.

I looked back at him. "Why would I do that? If Ryder's not here now, he's probably not coming."

Todd shrugged lightly. "You never know. We can wait together."

I made a calculation. It was better if Todd didn't think I suspected anything of him, so I shrugged. "Okay, might as well. If we've got Wi-Fi, the cable's probably working."

He cast me a lopsided grin, and for a second, he

was my brother's teasing friend from high school.

"True story. I can't remember the last time I was here."

"Probably in high school with us," I said casually as I stood and walked down the dark hallway toward the front of the house.

I took that moment to check the time on Russell's message. He'd left it while I was in the air and said they should be landing in Seattle around seven thirty. I did the math in my brain. By the time they landed and got a rental, it would be nine o'clock before they got here. That was two hours away. I only hoped I could play it cool for that long with Todd.

"Why don't I go get us some pizza at the store in town?" I prompted a few minutes later after checking in the kitchen and discovering not much of anything other than a few energy bars and some soda. "Do you drink anything other than soda?"

Todd shrugged. "The water's off. I thought about turning it on, but I thought maybe that wasn't the best move."

"No, that's a whole process. It's town water, so they have to call out before they come and get it turned on."

Todd was studying me quietly, and I hoped I looked completely oblivious.

"Pizza sounds like a good plan. I'll sit tight."

"What kind of pizza do you want?" This conversation felt so weird. It was about nothing important, yet the tension was coiled tightly inside me, so tight that my chest hurt.

"Meat lovers, that's my fave."

"We'll do half and half," I said.

He rolled his eyes. "Hell no. Get me a whole pizza and get whatever you want for yourself." He reached into his pocket, fishing out his wallet and handing me two twenty-dollar bills.

I left, almost gasping with relief once I started my car and backed out. I couldn't tell if my anxiety was better or worse once I was out of the house. It was only after I was halfway to town that I decided to call Russell and leave a return message explaining the current situation.

## Chapter Thirty-Two
# RUSSELL

I glanced over at Paisley's brother. "She's at your family's vacation place, and your friend is there. Why the fuck didn't you warn her about him?"

"He won't hurt her," Ryder said quickly.

"Are you sure about that?" I was furious and strung tight with worry.

"Look, I know he won't hurt her," he insisted.

"You better fucking be right. Now, do you want me to call her back?"

"When did she leave the message?" he asked.

"Right as we were landing."

"I don't want you to call if she's at the summer house."

He was driving, and we were zooming down the highway. Ryder had insisted on driving because he knew where he was going. Even though I'd wanted to argue, he had a point.

"If she left around twenty minutes ago and was headed to pick up pizza, where would she be now?" I asked.

"Probably at the pizza place."

"I'm calling."

I tapped the screen to return her call, and Paisley answered on the second ring. Relief slammed through me, seizing my breath in my lungs for a moment.

"Paisley! Where are you?"

"I'm at the pizza place," she explained. "I was trying to decide if I should stay here or go back to the summer house."

"I'm with your brother. Please stay at the pizza place."

"I'm a little worried that if I don't go back, Todd's going to wonder where I am. How far away are you guys?"

I moved the phone away from my mouth. "ETA?"

"About forty minutes, and that's if we don't get pulled over for speeding."

Paisley heard his answer and replied, "If I wait that long, he's definitely going to wonder."

"Paisley, I don't want you to go back there."

"Todd won't hurt me," she insisted.

"People do weird shit when they feel like they're in over their head."

She didn't respond to that. "You need to tell Ryder our father knows what's up. Just put me on speaker, so I can explain."

I did as she asked, lifting the phone away from my ear and holding it in my palm. "Paisley has something to tell you," I said as I glanced at him.

Her voice came through the speaker, and my heart clenched. "Dad knows, Ryder. He hasn't told Mom because he's hoping you'll do the right thing. Also, it doesn't look like we'll be doing anything fun for Mom and Dad's anniversary."

"Fuck," Ryder hissed. He bounced his fist lightly on the steering wheel. "And what's the right thing?"

"He's off the case, and they've told him they'll negotiate a deal with you if you testify. If you're wondering, I didn't tell him anything. He figured it out on his own."

I watched as her brother clenched a fist and released it. "I'm gonna have to figure out what to do, but right now, I don't want you to go back to the summer house."

"What's Todd going to do? He knows where I am, and he knows what I'm driving."

"Stay put, or go to the grocery store. Just go somewhere public," her brother replied.

"You're an asshole. You know that, right?" Paisley responded, her voice tight. "What the hell is going on? I got that call from Todd, and I'm stressing about you."

"Paisley, I couldn't tell you what was going on. I didn't want you to know everything. I sure as hell didn't think you were going to hop on a plane from Alaska and try to do something by yourself. What the fuck were you thinking?"

"What the hell, Ryder?" she countered. I could hear the tears in her voice, and my heart ached. "This whole thing is a mess, and I just want you to be okay. I'm not going to go back to the summer house. I'm starving, so I'll eat here. After that, I'll go to the grocery store or something. What are you going to do?"

"Go talk to Todd."

"Why don't you call Dad?"

"And let the police deal with us? Because Todd's my friend," Ryder replied quietly.

"Yeah, but you're both in over your head, I think," Paisley replied, her voice softening. "Can you put me off speaker, Russell?"

I immediately did as she asked and lifted the phone to my ear. "You okay?" I asked immediately.

"Not really. I want to talk, but not right now."

"Same here, but we're in the middle of a situation right now."

"We are."

"What do you want me to do?" I asked.

"Can you keep my brother from doing anything stupid?"

"You got it."

It was on the tip of my tongue to tell Paisley I loved her, but now didn't feel like the time.

"So let's talk later after this whole thing is sorted out, okay?"

"Definitely. I'll talk to you soon."

After we ended the call, I slipped my phone into my pocket. I stared ahead at the highway, watching the lines as they rolled by while I gathered my thoughts. "Here's the thing. I'm not gonna let you call the shots tonight. Maybe I don't have all the details on how you ended up in this fucked-up situation, but for once, you need to do the right thing for Paisley, for yourself, for your father, and for your friend, even if he's not thinking clearly. Call your father, figure out who you need to call, and then put a stop to this right now."

Her brother was dead silent for a full two minutes before he finally said, "Okay."

I was wound too tight with worry to relax. "I think I know Paisley pretty well, but obviously, you've known her longer than me. Do you think she'll stay away from the summer house, or will she go back anyway?"

"Paisley's sensible, so I think she'll stay away until she hears otherwise from us. I don't think Todd would do anything to hurt her, but he might try to use her for leverage. It's definitely best for her not to be there."

He reached for his phone, where it was resting in the cup holder between the seats. I listened while he called his father and then called someone else. The car ride felt endless. I was annoyed, and my heart ached. I was mostly tied up in knots with worry for Paisley. Because until I knew she was okay, she wasn't okay. I also knew she was torn up over what was going on with her brother. I was relieved her brother was doing the right thing.

Until I heard him say, "Excuse me, what? Fuck. I'm going there."

"What the fuck is going on?" I asked as his phone clattered into the cupholder.

## Chapter Thirty-Three
# RUSSELL

An hour later, with my heart pounding and my stomach tied up in knots, I waited down the road while the police dealt with the situation at Paisley's parents' vacation home. As far as I knew, Todd was refusing to come out. As Paisley had predicted, he'd gotten suspicious when she didn't return and found her at the pizza place. From what we understood, Paisley had played it cool and returned with him after alerting the staff at the pizza place to call the police when she went to the restroom.

The police had spoken to Paisley and said she was safe. I looked at her brother. "This is on you, you know."

Ryder leaned his head back against the seat, letting out a ragged sigh. "I fucking know, dude."

"What were you thinking?"

"I was young and stupid. Then I thought I could just keep it going and keep it controlled."

"Look, I know something about doing dumb shit when you're in college, but this is next level when you're committing crimes like this. All those people care about is the money. They're not going to protect you. They're going to protect the money. What made you and your friend think you could gracefully exit? Maybe he was your friend once, but right now, staying out of jail is more appealing to him."

"Obviously, I see that now," he muttered, leaning forward and running his hands roughly through his hair.

Rain ran down the windshield, blurring the view. We got sick of listening to the sound of the wipers, so we turned them off. It felt like forever before a police officer approached the car.

"We're still dealing with your friend, but Paisley's safe," the officer said through the window.

"Where is she?" I demanded.

"She's waiting up the road by her rental car." He glanced at Ryder. "You need to come with me."

"Can I talk to her?" I asked the officer.

At his nod, I stepped out in the rain, oblivious to it as it poured down over me. I followed where the officer pointed while he led Ryder over to a cluster of people standing near a police vehicle. Paisley was waiting beside a vehicle under an umbrella. She was talking to a police officer, and I didn't even notice. I ran to her, pulling her into my arms. She didn't hesitate, wrapping her arms tightly around my waist and burying her head against my chest.

## Chapter Thirty-Four
## PAISLEY

Russell's arms closed around me, and I pressed my face to his chest. I breathed in his familiar scent and tried to calm the emotion rushing through me. It was pouring outside, and I couldn't tell if my face was wet from tears or the rain.

I heard the rumble of Russel's voice, my name barely reaching me through the cacophony in my brain.

"Paisley," he repeated.

I lifted my head, peering up at him. His face was shadowed in the rainy darkness. "Let's get you in the car," he said. "Is this your rental?"

In another moment, he had guided me into the car after saying something to one of the police officers nearby. I huddled in the passenger seat, my arms curled around my waist while he started the car and turned the heat on full blast.

"How long have you been waiting?" he asked.

I wiped my palms across my cheeks. He reached over and opened the glove box, fishing out some tissues. I dabbed at my face and blew my nose. When

I finally looked at him, I promptly burst into tears again. He looked so concerned and worried, and this was all too much.

"I missed you," I said, between sniffles and hiccups.

"I missed you too."

The console was in the way. He slid his seat back as far as it would go before reaching over and pulling me onto his big, comforting lap. I savored that he was a tall, strong guy. I wasn't usually weepy, but at this moment, I was. I rested against his chest and cried for a few minutes.

He held me quietly. His warmth and the warm air blowing from the heat vents eventually began to seep through me, and I stopped shivering.

"What are you crying about?" he finally asked.

"I missed you," I whispered.

Apparently not loudly enough because he prompted, "You're crying because you missed me?"

I nodded against the curve of his neck. "That and the stupid mess my brother made."

"They're arresting Todd," he said.

"Are they arresting my brother?"

"I don't actually know," Russell replied, and I finally lifted my head. "He called your father on the way here, and then he called the prosecutor your father told him to call."

"Good," I said firmly. The relief washing through me was so immense it felt as if I were hollow inside. The absence of the ball of tension and worry I'd been carrying felt strange. "You have no idea how relieved I am," I added fervently. I blinked and took a breath. "You probably think I should've turned him in."

He shook his head slowly. "No, you love your brother. You stumbled into his secret, and you didn't know what to do with it. It was more complicated by the fact that your dad's the DA in your hometown."

"Oh, it's complicated all right," I said, my voice cracking.

Russell's palm moved in slow circles on my back. "Why'd you message me?" he finally asked.

It took more nerve than I was prepared for to tell him how I felt. I'd gone and fallen in love with this man, and I absolutely hadn't planned on it. Not even a little. "Because I'm in love with you."

"You are?" His lips quirked in a self-deprecating smile.

"Yes. Maybe that's weird to tell you now, but I missed you, and then I got worried, and everything started to stress me right the hell out. How did you get down here so fast?"

Russell shrugged. "It helps to have the right friends. You know Alex Blake?"

"I think I met him."

"He's an airplane mechanic and knows people at the airport in Anchorage. He happened to know there was a private business flight going from Anchorage to Seattle, and they let us hitch a ride," he explained.

"How does that even work?"

"You don't need tickets or anything. We were in the back, and we minded our own business. It was quicker than taking a commercial flight because we didn't have to wait."

I nodded, thinking this night could've gone differently if they hadn't gotten here so fast. "Where are you staying? I need to talk to my parents, but I don't want to stay there." All I wanted was to be with Russell.

"Let's stay at a hotel in Seattle," Russell prompted.

"Let me find out what's happening with my brother before we do anything."

"We can try, but I don't know how much we can find out tonight. Let me get an update. You stay in here. You're still cold."

We looked at each other for a minute. My heart was in my throat. He palmed my cheek and dipped his head for a kiss, claiming my mouth possessively and boldly. Another moment later, I was feeling breathless when he drew away.

"I'll be right back," he murmured.

I shimmied across the console and back into the passenger seat, holding my hands out in front of the heaters. I watched as he dashed into the rain and conferred with a few people. I could see my brother standing there. A part of me wanted to talk to him, but I just wasn't ready. All I needed to know was that he was safe. We could handle the rest later.

A few minutes later, Russell climbed back into the car. "Your brother's going with the police. I don't think he's officially arrested, but something's happening. He said to tell you he's sorry and he's fine. Todd's already cuffed."

"Wow. All right." Pausing, I took a slow breath as I absorbed the news. "Do you mind if I call my parents?"

"Of course not. Tell me a good hotel in Seattle first. That way, I can start driving."

I thought for a minute and then gave him the name of a place. "I'll put it in my maps and follow the friendly GPS voice, if you don't mind," he added.

"Go for it. We'll figure out our flight back to Alaska tomorrow."

Russell started driving, and once he was on the highway, I called my parents.

"Hi, Paisley," my father answered. "I already know the status, and your mom's right here."

"Is she okay?"

"Let me put you on speaker."

"Hey, Mom," I said a moment later.

"Hello, Paisley. Are you okay?"

"I'm fine. Are *you* okay?" I pressed.

"Well, I'm a little shaken and rattled and really upset with your brother, but I'm glad you're both safe."

I could tell from her voice that she'd been crying, and my heart pinched. "Are you sure you're okay, Mom?"

The sound of her shaky sigh was audible through the phone line. "I've known for a while something was off with your brother, but I didn't know what. I suppose a mother's intuition is a good indicator. I'm relieved, but I'm also furious. I'm not upset with you at all, and you need to know that. I understand why you didn't know what to do."

"Are you sure?"

"Absolutely, honey. You're not your brother's keeper," she said softly.

"Do you know anything else, Dad?" I asked.

"As you know, I'm no longer handling the case. If he helps the prosecution out with useful, verifiable information on the larger case, he'll probably manage a decent deal with them. He has not committed any violent crimes, which will help him a lot. Todd has a little more to answer for, but that's not our problem. Sometimes, people get in over their head, and it snowballs."

"That's one way to put it," I said dryly. Now that my brother was okay and the weight of his secret was lifted, I was starting to feel normal inside.

"Are you coming here tonight?" my mother asked.

"No, I'm with Russell, my boyfriend. We're going to stay at a hotel in Seattle and then fly back to Alaska. If you want, I can come by tomorrow. I just don't have it in me to drive there tonight."

"We understand. We'd love to see you soon, though," my mother interjected.

"I was hoping we could do something for your anniversary, which is coming up soon."

I felt my mother's smile through the line. "It is, but you know we're not big on *big* events."

I smiled to myself. "I know you're not, but it means a lot."

"We'll come up and visit soon, and you can take us out for dinner," my father added.

"I'd love that. I love you both."

"We love you too."

I tapped to end the call and glanced over at Russell. "Boyfriend?" His tone had a subtle teasing hint to it, but his gaze sobered quickly.

"What do you think you are?" I teased in return, so relieved to be able to tease about anything.

"At least that," he said.

My heart flipped over, and I felt a pull in the center of my chest.

He reached over to lace his fingers with mine as he kept one hand on the steering wheel and drove through the rainy darkness.

When we got to the hotel, my clothes were still damp, as were his. After we made it to the room, Russell dropped his bag on the floor and gestured to the bathroom. "Shower."

"Just me?"

"Oh no, I'm coming too, but you're still shivering, so get in there quick."

Following instructions, I hurriedly peeled off my damp clothes, leaving them in a messy pile on the bathroom floor. A few minutes later, we had water raining down around us, but this time, it was hot and steamy.

Russell's hands lathered the soap over my body. Before I knew it, he was kissing me, and I forgot the tension and fear that had dominated the day and how much I'd missed him. I let myself get lost in his kisses and the way he knew my body so well. He coaxed me to a climax with his fingers, and then he lifted me in his arms and pressed my back to the tiled wall. When he filled me, he held still, saying, "Paisley."

I dragged my eyes open. His dark gaze held mine. "Did I mention I missed you?" he murmured, his voice a husky whisper.

"You did," I whispered in return. "I need to tell you something."

"Can I go first?" he asked.

My heartbeat was thundering so hard I could barely hear over the blood rushing through my ears and the sound of the water falling around us in the shower. I nodded.

"I know things weren't supposed to get complicated, and we said no strings. I guess I lied. I fell in love with you."

My chest felt like it was going to explode. I blinked away the sting of tears in my eyes.

"You did?" I whispered over the thundering beat of my heart.

He nodded solemnly. "I didn't figure it out until you switched crews, and I got pissed. Then you left, and I panicked. Your brother figured it out before I did."

"You told him?"

Russell's lips curled in a self-deprecating smile. "He called me out on it, and I fessed up. Your brother might be stupid about some things, but apparently, he knows when someone loves you."

I lifted a hand, tracing my fingertips along his jawline. "I love you too. I panicked, and I thought you would think I was awful for what I was covering up for Ryder."

He shook his head. "Just like your dad said, it's not your job to keep your brother's secrets. It's not your fault what your brother does either."

"I know but—"

Russell cut me off with a quick kiss before lifting his head again. "I know you, Paisley. I'm sure this tore you up."

Wordlessly, I nodded.

"Where are you going to stay when we get back to Alaska?"

"With you," I replied, feeling my lips kick into a smile.

"It's a damn good thing you're going to stay with me." My heart felt full as joy radiated inside. "Somebody's got to cook for you."

"Hey, I might get better in the kitchen," I protested with a laugh.

This man, who held my heart in his hands, smiled one of his dangerous grins, and my stomach flipped. "I think you're a lost cause, but that's okay. I'll cook for you every day."

Then his mouth was on mine again, and he sent me flying.

# EPILOGUE
## Russell

I'd meant to make it a grand gesture, but that didn't work out in Seattle. I made up for the grand gesture later. I tried to persuade Paisley to switch back to Graham's crew with me when we got back to Alaska, but she flatly refused. Ward even backed up her logic.

Whatever. I wanted to have words with Ward about it, but I let it go.

Life stayed busy for both of us after we got back from our jaunt to help her brother. Paisley had spent far too much time worrying about him, and I was relieved he'd cooperated with the investigation after all was said and done. Since he hadn't committed any violent crimes, he managed to work out a deal for monitored probation.

On a more crucial matter, she moved back into the lake house with me. She had the better bedroom, so I stayed up there. My mother was over the moon about us. She even fessed up that Janet had suggested she offer the rental to Paisley because, apparently, Janet thought I had a thing for Paisley. She'd been spot on.

As for me? Tender was the only word I could come up with about my feelings.

I ran into Rowan one day in the parking lot at the station. He cracked a rare grin, commenting, "You seem to be in a better mood."

"I do?"

He chuckled. "Yeah. You're not being stupid anymore. Now, you better lock her down."

A full six months after his suggestion, I did. I got a ring and everything, and I made dinner—her favorite mac and cheese. Plus, a raspberry cheesecake. The first time I made it, she ate almost half of it by herself. I had it all planned. I even made it a surprise.

"Why am I wearing a blindfold?" she asked as I held her hand and led her into the kitchen.

"For fun," I teased.

Her lips were curled in a smile, and I bent low to kiss her when I stopped by the counter. We had already eaten the mac and cheese and gone for a walk. Her eyes flew wide when she saw the raspberry cheesecake. "Ooh! I didn't know if you were ever going to make it again."

"Of course, I was going to make it again."

"If you make this all the time, I will turn into a butterball."

I chuckled. She didn't need to worry about that. Hotshot firefighting was *not* an easy job and pretty much made it impossible to put on any weight.

"Let's eat dessert," I murmured, nudging her in the direction of the table.

She was several bites in when she started to sink her fork in, and it came to an abrupt stop, making a little clicking sound. Her eyes flew wide. "What's this?"

I waited. She carefully pushed the top layer away

to see the small glass box, and nestled inside of it was a ring. I'd cut a hole in the cake from the bottom to hide the box in there. She carefully smoothed her fork over the top. When she looked over at me, her eyes were glistening with tears. "Seriously? Are you asking me to marry you?"

"Yes, I am," I said flatly.

She sat completely still, long enough that I started to worry. When she lifted her eyes to mine again, she knuckled away the tears slipping down her cheeks.

"Russell. Oh, my God. Are you sure?"

"Am I sure that I love you? Yes. Am I sure that I want to spend the rest of my life with you? Yes, absolutely. Was this too soon?"

She shook her head, her hair swinging around her shoulders with the motion. "I love you." She leaped out of her chair, raced around the table, and slipped into my lap.

A moment later, she pressed her forehead to mine. "You surprised me," she whispered.

"You're not easy to surprise. I wanted to make it good."

I felt the curve of her smile on my cheek. "Maybe you can teach me how to make the cheesecake."

"No," I said firmly. Our last episode in cooking lessons for Paisley had not gone so well. She was too impatient and skipped too many steps. "I love you. You're the best roommate I've ever had."

"Am I still just your roommate?" she teased.

"Well, you're my roommate with benefits, and I love you. And now, you're my fiancée, and pretty soon, you'll be my wife. You're mine."

"Since when did you become a possessive guy?" she teased.

"Since you," I said bluntly before sliding my hand into her hair and holding her close.

Want a glimpse of the future for Russell & Paisley? Join my newsletter to receive an exclusive scene:

Sign up here: https://BookHip.com/GKXAXZA

p.s. If you are already subscribed, you'll still be able to access the scene.

Thank you for reading Paisley & Russell's story - I hope you loved it!

Up next in the Light My Fire Series is Only Ever Us. Rowan & Mae were best friends once. Young and reckless, they risked their friendship with a few dates. Just when they almost had it all, Mae cut Rowan out of her life.

She never told him why, and he never stopped loving her. When he takes a job as a hotshot firefighter in her small hometown in Alaska, he hopes he might finally find the answers.

Don't miss Rowan & Mae's hot, emotional second chance romance!

Pre-order Only Ever Us - due out Dec 14, 2021!

For more swoon-worthy small town romance...

This Crazy Love kicks off the Swoon Series - small town southern romance with enough heat to melt you! Jackson & Shay's story is epic - swoon-worthy & intensely emotional. Jackson just happens to be Shay's brother's best friend. He's also *seriously* easy on the eyes. Shay has a past, the kind of past she would most definitely like to forget. Past or not, Jackson is about to rock her world. Don't miss their story! Free on all retailers!

Burn For Me is a second chance romance for the ages. Sexy firefighters? Check. Rugged men? Check. Wrapped up together? Check. Brave the fire in this hot, small-town romance. Amelia & Cade were high school sweethearts & then it all fell apart. When they cross paths again, it's epic - don't miss Cade's story! Free on all retailers!

For more small town romance, take a visit to Last Frontier Lodge in Diamond Creek. A sexy, alpha SEAL meets his match with a brainy heroine in Take Me Home. Marley is all brains & Gage is all brawn. Sparks fly when their worlds collide. Don't miss Gage & Marley's story!
Free on all retailers!

If sports romance lights your spark, check out The Play. Liam is a British footballer who falls for Olivia, his doctor. A twist of forbidden heats up this swoon-worthy & laugh-out-loud romance. Don't miss Liam & Olivia's story.
Free on all retailers!

# FIND MY BOOKS

**Thank you for reading Hold Me Now! I hope you enjoyed the story. If so, you can help other readers find my books in a variety of ways.**

1) Write a review!
2) Sign up for my newsletter, so you can receive information about upcoming new releases & receive a FREE copy of one of my books: http://jhcroixauthor.com/subscribe/
3) Like and follow my Amazon Author page at https://amazon.com/author/jhcroix
4) Follow me on Bookbub at https://www.bookbub.com/authors/j-h-croix
5) Follow me on Instagram at https://www.instagram.com/jhcroix/
6) Like my Facebook page at https://www.facebook.com/jhcroix

**Light My Fire Series**
Wild With You
Hold Me Now
Only Ever Us - coming December 2021!
Fall For Me - coming February 2022!
**Dare With Me Series**
Crash Into You
Evers & Afters
Come To Me
Back To Us
**Swoon Series**
This Crazy Love
Wait For Me
Break My Fall
Truly Madly Mine
Still Go Crazy
If We Dare
Steal My Heart
**Into The Fire Series**
Burn For Me
Slow Burn
Burn So Bad
Hot Mess
Burn So Good
Sweet Fire
Play With Fire
Melt With You
Burn For You
Crash & Burn
That Snowy Night
**Brit Boys Sports Romance**
The Play
Big Win
Out Of Bounds
Play Me

Naughty Wish

**Diamond Creek Alaska Novels**
When Love Comes
Follow Love
Love Unbroken
Love Untamed
Tumble Into Love
Christmas Nights

**Last Frontier Lodge Novels**
Take Me Home
Love at Last
Just This Once
Falling Fast
Stay With Me
When We Fall
Hold Me Close
Crazy For You
Just Us

# ACKNOWLEDGMENTS

I'm so grateful for you, my readers. There are only so many ways to thank you, but it bears repeating. Thank you for giving my books a chance.

My assistant, Erin, is forever managing the details behind the scenes for me. Gracious thanks to my editor for helping me polish Russell & Paisley's story and to Terri D. for making sure my characters have the same eye color throughout the story and more.

Najla Qamber continues to create stunning covers for me and does so with kindness and patience.

To my early readers who let me know about any stubborn errors, and to the bloggers who shout out my books and so many others - massive thanks!

Of course, thank you to my husband, and to my dogs who only interrupt me a few hundred times a day for pets.

xoxo

J.H. Croix

# ABOUT THE AUTHOR

USA Today Bestselling Author J. H. Croix lives in a small town in Maine with her husband and two spoiled dogs. Croix writes contemporary romance with sassy women and alpha men who aren't afraid to show some emotion. Her love for quirky small-towns and the characters that inhabit them shines through in her writing. Take a walk on the wild side of romance with her bestselling novels!

*Places you can find me:*
jhcroixauthor.com
jhcroix@jhcroix.com

facebook.com/jhcroix
instagram.com/jhcroix
bookbub.com/authors/j-h-croix